The Legends of Nod

The Legends of Nod

Book II

All for the Blood of Nightstorm

Being the second volume in the first saga
The Sword of Libran

A story from
The Epic of Prince Joryn

by

Glenn Slade Clark, Jr.

2019

The Legends of Nod, Book II:
All for the Blood of Nightstorm

Copyright ©2014, 2019 by Clark Ink, LLC
First Edition E-Book: July 2014
Second Edition Hardback: July 2019
Second Edition Trade Paperback: July 2019

Published by Clark Ink, LLC. All characters, situations, and other imaginings featured in this publication are purely fictitious and bear no intended likeness to actual persons either living or dead.

This novella was originally published as
The Legends of Nod #2 "All for the Blood of Nightstorm."

This edition has been revised and expanded by the author.

Cover art by Molly Fine.

ISBN: 978-1-61815-114-8

For the Lou Scheimer generation.

CONTENTS

DRAMATIS PERSONAE

Centaurus – An immortal being considered by most mortals to be one of the Twelve Great Gods of Nod, manifests as a male humanoid with a horse head and feathered wings; credited with introducing the bow and arrow to the people of Nod; known as the god of war

Ambassador Dorran Equus – Centaur male from the nomadic Caluman tribe, age thirty-eight years; son of Rinaulf and Gylanna Equus; widower of Kalibi Equus; father of Lute Equus; ambassador to the Imperial court of Nod, representing the Twelve Tribes of the centaurs; master of hand-to-hand combat; champion of the Caluman tribe; urged by the Lord Caluman to ally himself more closely with his friend Prince Joryn, after the young prince's successful peace accord with the Empire of Dragons

Princess Hero – Human female from the Kingdom of Nod, age twenty-six years; daughter of Emperor Sapros and Lady Leita; older sister of Prince Vail; younger half-sister of Prince Kail, Prince Repteré, Princess Willowyll, and Prince Dakarai; older half-sister of Prince Mwana, Princess Adaeze, Prince Dorago, Princess Enjinia, Princess Lily, and Prince Joryn

Sir Illium – Bionic unicorn male from the Golden Field, age 1,000 years; son of Ryjan and Maladine; husband of Lady Norlan; father of Charger; knight of the Order of the Golden Field; royal steed of Prince Joryn

Iron Bill – Deluvian war bird male, from the kingdom of Deluvia, age 4,588 years; son of Red Rodger and Dawn Glider; last of the Deluvian war birds

Prince Joryn – Human male from the Kingdom of Nod, age twenty years; youngest son of Emperor Sapros and the Unnamed Empress; younger brother of Prince Kail; youngest half-brother of Prince Repteré, Princess Willowyll, Prince Dakarai, Princess Hero, Prince Mwana, Princess Adaeze, Prince Dorago, Princess Enjinia, Prince Vail, and Princess Lily; paramour of Lord Galen; newly appointed champion of Libran; recently returned from a successful peace accord with the queen of the Empire of Dragons

Kabed – Human male from the kingdom of Deluvia, age twenty-four years; tech wizard; Imperial head of science for Emperor Sapros; inventor of Aeropacks and the robotic unicorns called Unitrons

Prince Kail – Human male from the Kingdom of Nod, age thirty-five years; eldest son of Emperor Sapros and the Unnamed Empress; older brother of Prince Joryn; eldest half-brother of Prince Repteré, Princess Willowyll, Prince Dakarai, Princess Hero, Prince Mwana, Princess Adaeze, Prince Dorago, Princess Enjinia, Prince Vail, and Princess Lily; husband of Princess Maressah; heir apparent to the thrones of both the Kingdom of Nod and the Empire of Nod; member of Emperor Sapros' Advisory Council

Lowgun Kin – Reptisaur male from the city of Slythe Orn, age 102 years; professional speedracer; owner of the *Dragon Racer*; outlaw, wanted dead or alive by the Mech Valley Authority

Ton La – Highland Elf male from the kingdom of the Highlands, age thirty-nine years; son of Blue and Sevien La; older brother of Leena La; husband of Prin La; warrior in the army of King Rune

Libran – An immortal being considered by most mortals to be one of the Twelve Great Gods of Nod, manifests as a male humanoid with white feathered wings; known as the god of balance, though he shuns the notion of godhood; has recently chosen Prince Joryn to serve the world of Nod as his champion

Longshot – Human male from the city of TexStar, age nineteen years; gunslinger; outlaw, wanted dead or alive by the Mech Valley Authority

Marley – Unitron (robotic unicorn), male gender identity programming, from the Kingdom of Nod, age two months; steed of Kabed; formerly known as Unitron 001

General Nightstorm the Merciless – Chirop male from the kingdom of Chiroptera, age fifty-three years; son of Ranshaarr and Aelbludd; lord of Nyx Bastion; general of the army of King Orlok

King Rune Ördo – Highland Elf male from the kingdom of the Highlands, age fifty-five years; son of King Burloe and Queen Mixtrah Ördo; older brother of Prince Dana Ördo; husband of Queen Jem Ördo; father of Prince Lothu Ördo, Prince Dun Ördo, and Prince Jarna Ördo

King Orlok the Unforgiven – Chirop male from the kingdom of Chiroptera, age fifty-six years; son of King Moonbreaker the Destroyer and Shadow Queen Ironfang; widower of Queen Sheerta; father of Prince Orlok the Younger, Prince Madblood, Prince Wildclaw, and Princess Nora; ruler of the kingdom of Chiroptera

(Miiko) Quickwing – Celestian male from the kingdom of Celestia, age twenty-eight years; son of Strongtide and Starsong; master of the broadsword; champion of the kingdom of Celestia; tasked by his uncle, Chief Sunray, to serve at the side of Prince Joryn

Emperor Sapros – Human male from the Kingdom of Nod, age sixty years; son of Emperor Barnard and Imperial Queen Mother Mideerma; older brother of Prince Bohmaine; widower of the Unnamed Empress; husband of Lady Makhaira, Lady Amina, Lady Leita, and Lady Riko; father of Prince Kail, Prince Repteré, Princess Willowyll, Prince Dakarai, Princess Hero, Prince Mwana, Princess Adaeze, Prince Dorago, Princess Enjinia, Prince Vail, Princess Lily, and Prince Joryn; ruler of both the Kingdom of Nod and the Empire of Nod

Shilo – Klomper male from the kingdom of the Highlands, age eighteen years; steed of Drae Shivvan

Drae Shivvan – Highland Elf male from the kingdom of the Highlands, age twenty-seven years; son of Burcher and Linelle Shivvan; older brother of Lin Shivvan; champion of the Highlands

Onri Sprigg – Lowland Elf male from Candy Village, age thirty-five years; son of Pipper and Nesta Sprigg; younger brother of Lesha Garmen and Kirna Figg; older brother of Zazu Sprigg; famous adventurer and swordsman; champion of the kingdom of the Lowlands; Onri's exploits in the Outer World have been famously chronicled in a trilogy of books by the renowned Lowland scribe, Dandy Jim; tasked by Governor Bumble Pepper to serve at the side of Prince Joryn

Priestess Tianna – Human female, age nineteen years; priestess of the Temple of Libran on the grounds of Palace Nod

Trig – Robotic horse/light gun, male gender identity programming, from the city of Mech Valley, age five years; steed of Longshot; outlaw, wanted decommissioned by the Mech Valley Authority

Prince Vail – Human male from the Kingdom of Nod, age twenty-two years; son of Emperor Sapros and Lady Leita; younger brother of Princess Hero; younger half-brother of Prince Kail, Prince Repteré, Princess Willowyll, Prince Dakarai, Prince Mwana, Princess Adaeze, Prince Dorago, and Princess Enjinia; older half-brother of Princess Lily, and Prince Joryn

The Legends of Nod

Book II

All for the Blood of Nightstorm

CHAPTER 1:
A WARRIOR'S BARGAIN

DRAE SHIVVAN OF THE HIGHLAND ELVES CREPT through the shadows of a dark and eldritch forest known as the Sea of Moss, on his way to a cave that only he knew existed. He had been making this same journey once a fortnight for the past five years, doing all in his power to avoid discovery.

Drae entered the cave, pushing aside the natural moss curtains that concealed it, and removed the dark green cloak that had helped him to blend into the shadows. He put aside his bow and touched a starjewel on the wall. The starjewel, true to its nature, came alive with light and began a chain reaction that lit the other

starjewels that had been placed in the cave by Shivvan years ago
to provide what little illumination was necessary to approach the
altar that he had built to the god Centaurus, who had given the
bow and arrow to the peoples of Nod in the distant days before
the Empire.

Drae knelt before the altar and prayed aloud, as he did during every such visit, hoping for a blessing; hoping for the great
god's mighty arms to join him. "Mighty Centaurus, I, Drae
Shivvan, truest warrior of the Highland Elves, beseech you once
again. I am yours from this day to the end of eternity. Just grant
me my heart's desire. Grant me the blood of Nightstorm.

"It is five years now, almost to the day, since that monster
took the life of my brother Lin, who I pray is safe and happy now
in the Land of Merigo. But I miss him, Centaurus." His face
contorted. Something was different. He felt his rage even more
potently than usual. "I *burn* with hatred for Nightstorm! Curse all
the Chirops! I will do *anything* to have my vengeance upon my
brother's killer. Anything you wish! Just ask it, Centaurus, and I
will submit."

Drae put his forehead down on the altar and shed tears, as
he did each time, letting them fall to the altar as his offering of
sincerity to the god of the archers.

"Drae Shivvan! The gods of Nod have heard your pleas!"

The elf fell back in horror, shielding his eyes from the powerful vision of Centaurus' face that hovered above his altar. "Ce
… Centaurus! My god!" His tears fell freely now, as he prostrated
himself before the being that embodied all of his darkest hopes.
"I am your servant."

"Yes. I know," said the god. "And you *will* pay the price. I will grant you the blood of Nightstorm. I will make it so that you will be the one who ends his life on the battlefield. But you must do something for me. Something that may not sit well with a noble warrior, but it is for the gods to understand what must be done, and it is for the creatures of Nod to obey."

On his knees, Drae vowed, "Anything, great Centaurus. Ask, and I will obey."

Pleased by the elf's willingness, Centaurus laid out his terms. "Just as you seek the blood of Nightstorm, I burn for the blood of Libran's champion, Prince Joryn, son of the human emperor Sapros."

Drae knew of Prince Joryn. The tale of his quest to bring peace between the Empire and the dragons had spread far and wide throughout the land of Nod in the past month. "My god, I will do whatever you ask, but how will I find such an opportunity? He is a prince in the Imperial Palace, the chosen hero of a god …"

"Do you doubt my assurance that I have the power to give you all that you ask of me?"

"No, Lord Centaurus."

"Then hear me. I will set the heart of King Orlok of Chiroptera on the crops of the Highland Elves. The Chirops will raid the farmlands and steal your people's food to the last grain. The Highlands will be left with nothing to store for the coming seasons of cold. Your king will send you to the emperor for support. You will urge Sapros to send an army to invade Chiroptera and take back what has been stolen. Surely the champion of Libran will join you in this battle, and you will have your opportunity to kill the Chirop who slew your brother. All I ask in return: see to it that Prince Joryn does not return home from the battle alive. Do you accept the terms of your god Centaurus?"

A thousand questions flooded Drae's mind. Why would Centaurus want Prince Joryn dead? What had the young prince done? What would become of Drae himself, if he slew the champion of all of Nod? Was it worth the trouble to become a villain, just to have Nightstorm's head? In little time at all, he reached his decision. "I agree to your terms, mighty Centaurus."

A powerful light knocked Drae Shivvan to his hands and knees. He cried out, fearing the light would destroy him. When the light was gone, Drae looked up, and he saw that the god had left him as well. He noticed a stinging sensation on his right arm. He looked down and saw a golden tattoo. The Mark of Centaurus. It sparkled in the sparse light of the starjewels.

"Soon, Lin, I will spill the blood of the monster who took you from me. No price could ever be too high."

As Drae Shivvan entered the capital city of the mountain kingdom of the Highland Elves several hours later, night had fallen in more ways than one. The people were in a panic. Drae noticed the silhouettes of hundreds of Chirops' wings spread against the starry sky. "So soon," he marveled.

"Drae! Drae! Thank the gods you're here! Where have you been?"

Drae took in the sight of his mother. She was in a state of sheer terror. He answered her, "I went into the forest to pray. I had a foreboding sense when I awoke this morning."

"Then the gods were trying to warn you! The Chirops attacked! They took everything! All of the farmers have either been killed or …"

Drae's heart nearly stopped. "Father?"

"I don't know, Drae! It was suicide to go down to the fields. I've been waiting for word, hoping they wouldn't come into the city."

Drae was running down the street towards the steep slopes that led to the farmers' fields before his mother had even finished speaking. He spotted his grazing klomper and quickly leapt onto its hard, unsaddled shell, urging it to run with all of the speed that its eight legs could manage. The klomper carried him to his father's field, and he saw the state of things. Everything was gone, just as Centaurus had promised, down to the last grain. His people had been left with absolutely nothing for the winter.

He saw his father, lying on the ravaged ground. He went to him, horrified, and tried to rouse him. The older elf's body was covered in blood. "Father, please!"

"I'm … Son? They came out of nowhere. They took everything. I … I tried to fight them off. But I …" He closed his eyes and said no more.

Drae carried him to the klomper and put him astride in front of himself. He patted the creature's hairy head and stroked the fur of its long neck with gratitude. "Carry us gently, Shilo, but still move fast. His breath has not yet left him."

The creature obeyed, and they made their way to the medic's hut. Drae carried his father in and noticed the massive number of wounded that were already in the doctor's care.

"How bad is he, Drae?" The doctor asked.

"He's still breathing, Zogra, but he's lost a lot of blood."

The doctor nodded. "I will put him first in line for you."

"Thank you." Drae carried his father to a mat on the floor and laid him down.

"No trouble," the doctor answered. "Anything for our greatest hero. I expect you'll be on your way to fix this?"

Drae nodded somberly. "With all speed." He took his father's hand and hoped the old elf could hear him in his sleep. "Fear not, Father. It will all be worth it in the end."

The doctor had time only to offer a puzzled look at the warrior's words before a contingent of the king's guard entered and addressed the kingdom's champion, "Drae Shivvan, King Rune sends for you at once."

Drae nodded and rose. "Take care of him, Zogra. I will make this right."

Drae was led into the throne room of the king of the Highlands. The king addressed him the moment he entered. "Drae, this is our darkest hour. The Chirops raped our fields without provocation. We've had nothing but peace with them for years. I had thought our skirmishes a thing of the past, but this is too great a line that they have crossed. Our people will starve."

"I agree, King Rune. We must take action immediately."

"Yes. That is why I am sending you with a delegation to Emperor Sapros to plead our case. I request the aid of the Empire in launching an outright invasion of Chiroptera. We will take back what they have stolen from us, and more."

Feeling elated, Drae bowed his head. "It is my honor to serve, my king. We will leave at once for the Palace of Nod."

Everything was transpiring in accordance with Centaurus' word.

CHAPTER 2:
A PLEA TO THE KINGDOM OF NOD

THE FOLLOWING MORNING, PRINCE JORYN WAS DEEPLY involved in a game of Imperial StrataGem with his recent acquaintance Onri Sprigg, hero of the Lowland Elves. Joryn was still not used to the hero worship that had followed his adventure with the dragons. Over the past month, various kingdoms within the Empire had sent their champions to join him in his implicit quest to protect the realm. Onri had been the second to arrive. Only two feet tall, the little warrior made up for his lack of height with a tremendous heart, full of courage, and a mouth so generally foul that even a giant might back away from the elf in a battle, out of sheer revulsion.

The first warrior to arrive had been Miiko Quickwing, from the cloud kingdom of Celestia. He was brawny to an extreme and a master of the broadsword. Quickwing's glorious, feathered wings made him, and all of the Celestians, appear very close in design to Libran himself.

Of course, the centaurs had already placed Dorran Equus in the palace to serve Emperor Sapros and represent their tribes in the emperor's court, but they now urged him to ally himself more with the young prince, which hadn't been hard for him to do, since they had already been great friends.

In all honesty, though Joryn had brought peace between the dragons and Imperial Nod, the young prince was feeling like a tremendous disappointment to his tacit new disciples. He felt that Quickwing and Onri especially had been expecting a life of battles and high adventure when they'd been sent to serve at his side. But the truth was, all that he'd done of any significance since they'd arrived was annihilate them at Imperial StrataGem. This seemed to vex Onri far more than Quickwing. The little warrior did not like to lose.

"I've got you now, you dirty, crotch-whiffing dog!" Onri moved his game piece on the board in a direct line towards the glowing starjewel in the center of the game board, taking down one of the prince's knights and anticipating victory.

"Interesting move," Joryn said dryly. He then moved his piece in a diagonal line, taking out three of Onri's knights, including the one right beside the gem.

Onri was incensed. "No! You won't beat me again! I'll be avenged this day! I will have your head!"

Joryn couldn't help but laugh, as the elf's pointed ears twitched in outrage and his face went red. "Ah, Onri. You shouldn't play so angry all the time. Maybe then you'd have a chance at beating me."

Miiko Quickwing, Dorran Equus, and the bionic unicorn Illium had been watching the game intently.

Joryn's oldest brother, Prince Kail, walked out into the courtyard where the game was taking place and laughed at the sight. "Again, Sprigg? When will you ever learn?"

The Lowland Elf grumbled. "I'm not here to learn, but to *teach*! As in teach this young fool a lesson."

"Uh … what lesson might that *be*, Onri?" Equus mocked. "That no matter how many times he beats you, he'll still be able to beat you again?"

"No! I will teach him that no one defeats Onri Sprigg without suffering unheard of vengeance!" Onri moved his game piece into position to wipe out Joryn's entire lineup.

Or so he thought.

Joryn moved the one piece Onri had been ignoring right up onto the gem. "Game."

"*What?*! No fair!"

"It's fair, Onri. I told you, you just play angry. You were so determined to kill my knights that you weren't putting any effort into guarding the gem."

"You cheat! I'll make you drink my dookie!"

The entire group laughed, even Illium, who added, "I would listen to Joryn's wisdom, Sprigg. He is the man who spoke with the queen of dragons and lived to tell the tale, after all."

There it was again. Joryn thought that he should feel proud every time that particular adventure came up, every time someone noticed the Sword of Libran at his side, but he didn't. Rather, he felt undeserving. Another game of StrataGem. Another mention of his heroic deeds. Another moment of wondering how disappointed these champions from across the Empire were in the lack of adventures to come. He felt like a fraud.

"What's wrong, Little Brother?" Kail asked. "You won! You should look happy, not morose."

Joryn sighed. "Nothing, Kail. I'm just … restless, I guess."

"Understood. It's been a quiet month."

"Too quiet," Joryn muttered.

Illium nudged the prince with his snout, trying to cheer him.

Joryn smiled in spite of himself. "I know, Illium, maybe we should go for a run through the plains."

Onri would not have it. "A run through the plains! Ha! How about another game, or are you too cowardly to face my wrath!" The elf was standing on top of the game table now, shaking his fist in the prince's face.

"Cowardly? I've beaten you exactly one-hundred *three* times now, Onri. What should I fear from you?" He laughed affectionately.

Onri hissed angrily, "Sweet revenge, you spineless, baby-eating, lizard molesting, sack of sh—"

"Onri!" Joryn cut the lowland elf off, a look of dismay coloring his face. "Where did you ever learn to hurl such insults? I've been wondering for some time."

"In a strange world, beyond our own. The world outside of Nod, where I had a trilogy of adventures!"

"A *trilogy?*" Illium asked.

"Yes, spike noggin! A *trilogy* of my own adventures, as chronicled by the great scribe Dandy Jim of the Lowland Elves: *Onri Sprigg and the Donut House of Doom, Onri Sprigg and the Cineplex of the Undead Teens*, and lastly *Onri Sprigg and the Deadly Cave of Be'Otch the Bear*! I'm a legend! A warrior to be feared throughout all the Lowlands! None there have *ever* beaten me in a game of Imperial StrataGem!"

Quickwing snickered, as he polished his sword on the railing overlooking the kingdom. "This 'trilogy' sounds like just the thing to aid my meditation. And, I suppose that a people who live in houses made of candy *would* be easily frightened."

"Don't bring up those friggin' candy houses, you feathery mother—"

"It's a game of strategy, Onri." Prince Kail put a hand on the elf's shoulder, deftly diffusing the situation. "One has to think with the brain, not emotions. That's how I taught Joryn to play when we were younger. It took him a long time to beat me too, but when he tried it my way, he actually started to win every now and again."

Onri Sprigg only grumbled. He then pronounced, "I starve! Let's adjourn to the kitchen!"

Equus agreed enthusiastically. "The ferocious elf of Candy Village is sheer genius! Let's do as he says."

Miiko Quickwing, still polishing his sword, shrugged easily. "I'm not hungry really. Wait a minute. Yes, I am. Let's go."

"If hunger is on your hearts, my friends," a new voice broke in, "then perhaps you are in the right state of mind to hear the plight of the Highland Elves."

Joryn stood, taken off guard by the appearance of the tall and lean warriors from the Highlands. "Who are you?" Noting with alarm that the group had not been announced, he demanded, "How did you get in past the guards?"

Prince Kail broke in more diplomatically, "I am Prince Kail, heir to the throne of Nod. This is my brother, Prince Joryn, and these are our friends, Illium, Dorran Equus, Quickwing, and Onri Sprigg. How may we help you this day?" He offered a smile, but beneath was a sense of wariness.

Drae Shivvan bowed, and the warriors in his company did likewise. "I am Drae Shivvan, champion of the mountain kingdom of King Rune. I seek an audience with King Sapros, Emperor of Nod." He eyed Joryn, astounded by his youth. *Could this really be the one who faced down the queen of dragons?* "As to how we got past the guards, my people have always been light of foot. They simply did not notice us or even try to prevent us entering the palace grounds."

"You spoke of the plight of the Highland Elves. I was not aware of any such troubles." Kail awaited the elf's reply.

"Surely not. It was only last night that we were invaded without provocation by the armies of Chiroptera. They stripped our fields bare, leaving us with nothing. Harvest nears, and our people will surely starve when the snow comes. The Chiropterans are many, and their wings give them the advantage. We seek the aid of the emperor in reclaiming what is ours."

Prince Kail nodded solemnly. "I will take you to my father."

***

As Kail entered the throne room, followed by Joryn and Drae Shivvan, his father was consulting with Tianna, the priestess of Libran. Kail noted the fact that his father had gained a new interest in the workings of Libran, since Prince Joryn's recent adventure. The emperor now seemed to be searching for something in the lore of the so-called god of balance, as if sizing up an enemy.

The ruler of Nod and the priestess looked to the new arrivals. "Well, what is this?" the emperor addressed his eldest son.

"A visitor from the Highland Elves," Kail said. "I present the warrior Drae Shivvan, with an urgent request for aid from King Rune."

King Sapros, Emperor of Nod, looked to the new arrival. "Then speak."

Tingling to the tips of his pointed ears with anticipation of the vengeance to come, Drae moved a few steps forward and told the emperor of his people's plight. "Your Majesty, if I may speak right to the point, the people of Chiroptera attacked our farmland in the Highlands without warning or provocation. We have had nothing but peace with these creatures for the past five years, but now they leave us with nothing to harvest for the coming cold. Indeed, they have stripped our crops down to the last grain. King Rune sends me to speak on his behalf, in hopes that our emperor may lend us some of his strength in the unavoidable conflict; for we must invade Chiroptera and reclaim what is ours, or our people will surely starve."

"Have you come alone?" asked Emperor Sapros, ever suspecting a trap or a trick, even from the most honest of his subjects.

"I have not. Prince Kail wisely suggested that my contingent await me outside. I am not here to force the issue, but to beg, if I must, as a humble servant of my emperor."

Sapros considered. He then punched a button on the arm of his throne and spoke, so that the device near his head on the throne would carry his voice to another room. "Golan, get King Orlok on the screen in my throne room. *Immediately!*"

"Yes, Your Majesty," came the filtered-sounding voice from the other room.

King Sapros huffed. "We will soon see this matter resolved, one way or another."

After a moment, the voice of Golan returned. "My king, I'm afraid King Orlok will not take your call."

"*What?*"

"His operator tells me the king is not to be disturbed."

"I am the *Emperor of Nod!*" Red-faced, the king railed on. "I want that Chirop operator on the screen in my throne room *now!*"

"Yes, Your Majesty."

An instant later, a bat-faced humanoid appeared on the wall, larger than life. "I told you, King Orlok does not wish to be dist—"

"Refuse my underlings if you dare it, but do not refuse *me*, you simpering idiot!"

Startled and terrified, the Chirop operator stammered, "K-k-king Sapros! Your Majesty, I thought it was Golan again."

"Put me through to King Orlok, idiot, and do it *now!*"

"Well, Y-Y-Your Majesty, as I already told your operator, the king won't take your call." The bat-like Chirop looked as though he wanted to hide under a rock.

Emperor Sapros stood and went even redder in the face than he'd already been. "Your King Orlok is *not* my equal! None in all of boundless Nod are my equal! I am the *Emperor* of Imperial Nod, and I will speak with your fool of a monarch now, or he will face my *immeasurable* displeasure!"

If Chirops could sweat, the poor operator on the screen would have been doing so profusely. "I have been instructed, Your Majesty, to r-r-remind you that Chiroptera is not a part of your empire."

"Your fool king has one hour to return my call," Sapros retorted, "or I will send in an army to reclaim the crops of the Highland Elves by force. You may in fact *become* a part of my empire through your king's stupidity!"

"I-I-I'll r-r-relay the message, Your Majesty. G-g-good day." The Chirop operator signed off, and the screen went blank.

Emperor Sapros looked to the Highland Elf. "You will have your aid. If Orlok does not contact me within an hour, the forces of Palace Nod will be at your side."

He looked predatorily at his youngest son. "Joryn, *hero* of Nod. Ready my troops. *You* will lead them into battle alongside the forces of King Rune, at his pleasure."

Drae eyed the young prince, his unwitting payment to the god Centaurus. *Can it really be so easy? The sacrificial youth has been handed to me!*

Kail shot his younger brother a worried glance. "Father, if it pleases you, I volunteer to accompany Joryn on this quest. He's never led the—"

"No!" Sapros cut him off. "You are my heir. I'll not risk you on the front lines against such terrible foes as the Chirops."

But you don't mind risking me, do you, old man? Joryn thought. *Or is it no risk at all to lose me?* "Father," he said aloud, "Kail is right. I'm grateful for your confidence in me, but I'm no general."

The emperor laughed viciously. "*You?* Not ready? Nonsense, oh Joryn Peace-Bringer! The deadly mountains of Chiroptera should be as nothing for a mighty hero such as yourself! Merely wave at them with the splendorous glory of the Sword of Libran, and they'll bow down to you as our ancient enemies the dragons did! The Chiropterans' ability to fly, their gruesome weapons, their legendary thirst for human blood, should be as nothing to you, oh Champion of Libran! I shall have our priestess of that grand old god say a blessing over you before you depart."

Beside the throne, Tianna bowed slightly to Joryn.

Hurt by the bitter hatred in his father's voice, Joryn nodded. "I will not fail you, Father."

"Whatever the outcome of this battle, I shall not be disappointed ..." as an afterthought, the king added, "... by the courage of my son." The Emperor of Nod smiled malevolently and waved a hand. "See to your preparations. I'm sure your band of elite followers will be thrilled to see their muse back in action."

Drae spoke then, "You have the thanks of King Rune."

The emperor grunted with a nod and repeated the dismissive wave of his hand.

The three men bowed and left the room.

***

"He hates me. He wants to see me killed," Joryn whispered to his brother, as they returned to the courtyard, where Drae's contingent and Joryn's friends had been waiting patiently.

One of the elf warriors had engaged in a game of StrataGem with Dorran the centaur, but they both forgot their game when they saw that Drae and the two Imperial princes had returned.

Kail was visibly haunted by the behavior of his father towards his brother. "He fears you. Ever since your return."

"It's getting worse. If the Chirops don't kill me, he may even kill me himself."

Kail sighed. "He hasn't yet. And he's the emperor. What's to stop him?"

They walked into the sunlight, and all the warriors in the courtyard went silent, awaiting news of the emperor's decision.

When Prince Kail said nothing, Joryn looked to him and mumbled quietly, "Well? Tell them already."

Kail spoke just as quietly, "The mission is yours, and these men are your followers. I will leave you to it. Show them strength and confidence, or they'll only doubt themselves." He patted his brother's shoulder, then turned and left the courtyard.

Joryn braced himself and addressed the gathered warriors. "We await a response from Chiroptera. If they've not replied in an hour, we march on their mountain with the Highland Elves."

The warriors cheered.

Illium remained silent of course. Unicorns were well known for their composure.

"At last!" Miiko Quickwing crowed, holding aloft his polished, deadly blade. "My sword has long thirsted for the blood of the vile bat folk!"

Joryn felt a chill at the declaration. It was all wrong. This invasion was wrong. He was not a spiller of blood. If he had been, he would have died in Din, when he had spoken with the queen of dragons. He had been hailed a hero for his actions, but his ways were quite different from the ways of these warriors who had been sent to follow him. He was a peaceful warrior, and he doubted these champions would understand that the term was not at all paradoxical. He doubted his ability to lead them.

As if reading his mind, Illium caught his eye and winked reassuringly.

Joryn nodded, his heart catching in his throat, as he prepared to disillusion his followers. "I have been placed in charge of this invasion," he spoke above the cheers, and they died down to hear his words, "and not a single life shall be taken under my command."

Stunned silence greeted him, until Onri Sprigg gave voice to Joryn's greatest fears. "What? You pants-pissing coward! How are we to take back what the monsters have stolen if we don't lop off some heads!"

More stunned silence, this time directed at the elf who dared to insult the emperor's son so harshly. Joryn wondered if the elfin warrior had merely spoken the words that no one else had dared.

Angered, he spoke firmly, "I am no coward, Onri Sprigg. I tell you that the victory I found with the dragons, which you all claim to hold in such high esteem, and the favor of Libran, who gave me his sword and shield, were won in this way. Though I wear Libran's sword at my side, it is merely a symbol. My true sword is my spirit, and it has won victory where all others have failed. So, I say again, we will invade Chiroptera if we must, but we will not take a single life. All light guns will be set to stun.

"If you'd rather not follow my philosophy, you are free to return to the Candy Village, Onri. None will think you a coward for it. I will leave you now to prepare our troops. If you are still here when I return, I will be honored to have you fighting by my side." Joryn turned then and left them, followed quickly by loyal Illium.

Onri Sprigg stood stunned at the prince's rebuke. "I'm not a coward," he said weakly to any who would hear him. "I will stay."

Miiko Quickwing watched the young prince striding away in the distance. "My people, in the cloud world of Celestia, are fierce warriors when they have to be. I should know. I am the greatest of them. But I must say, it's always troubled me. Our way of war doesn't hold with our spiritual teachings. Above all, we of Celestia are a spiritual people, at one with nature. If Joryn wants to try to wage war in this way, I will follow his lead. I feel the Great Spirit would approve. Prince Joryn is a *great* warrior who has never taken a life. I have no doubts in my pledge to follow him."

"I agree." Onri was humbled. "I should not have spoken to him in that way. Do you think he'll now count me among his enemies?"

Dorran laughed and smacked the StrataGem table with the massive palm of his hand. "Oh, he'll still have your back in battle, shorty. He's as good as his word. But, if you'd reconsider and depart, I'll offer you a ride on my back. I wouldn't mind a taste of this Candy Village you hail from."

His anger rekindled, the elf shook a fist in the centaur's direction. "Do not *speak* to me of candy, you pantless weirdo!"

"*That's* my Onri!" Dorran bellowed joyously. "Now let's go find some food. We've quite a ways to travel, should the Chirops fail to cooperate."

As Joryn's entourage made their way to the dining hall, Drae Shivvan followed with his men in silent contemplation. This Prince Joryn was one unexpected revelation after another. So young and fair, so bold and wise. None of it quite fit with what he'd been expecting. This *peaceful warrior* was a truly good man, and his reputation well earned. It pained Drae, the thought of leading him to his untimely end, but any second thoughts were quickly brushed away by the knowledge that the death of Prince Joryn would finally allow him to avenge his brother's death. Could he kill a fellow hero in pursuit of Nightstorm's blood? He realized he really had no choice. He rubbed his arm and the golden Mark of Centaurus that now branded it. The deal was done. It would all be worth it, when Nightstorm, at last, lay dying at his feet.

As the warriors ate, Prince Joryn sat outside the dining hall, contemplating his predicament. He was brought out of his reverie by the approach of Tianna, the mystical priestess of Libran.

"Dark thoughts, my prince?"

He smiled at the words of his longtime friend. "No. Just … thoughts. This is a very unexpected quest that I am about to endure. I'm just wondering whether or not I can pull it off."

The priestess nodded. "I was watching, from the shadows, when you addressed the warriors in the courtyard. They will follow you. They were surprised by your stand, but they respected it deeply. You have nothing to fear from those who have pledged themselves to you."

He nodded thoughtfully. "Why do I sense a *but*?"

"Always the perceptive one," she confessed. "I do not trust this warrior from the Highlands. He is telling the truth, of that I am certain. *But* … there is something he's concealing. Something about him does not sit right with me. I wish I could place it."

"Well, we leave as soon as the troops are ready. If it hasn't come to you by then, contact us the moment that it does. Meanwhile, I will take heart in the fact that Drae Shivvan is telling us the truth."

Tianna nodded, then ventured another matter-of-fact observation, "Something else is troubling you."

"Yes." Joryn looked wistfully to the horizon, in the direction of the Whispering Plains. "I just … wish Galen were here. His love is the one strength I feel might carry me into this ordeal with a sense of invincibility."

Tianna put a hand to Joryn's chest. "He *is* with you, Joryn. He thinks of you as often as you think of him. There is no reason you shouldn't take his love with you *wherever* you go."

Joryn beamed. "Long distance relationships … I'm glad to hear you so certain about this."

"It's written in his eyes whenever he visits, just as it is written in yours."

Joryn grabbed her then and kissed her on the forehead. "Bless you, Tianna. I shall carry his love into battle as my armor and your certainty as my shield." He lowered his arms and shrugged. "I'd better go and see Kabed. He may have some more practical ideas on how to make this bloodless invasion work."

"Of that," Tianna agreed with a smile, "I have no doubt."

Kabed's workshop was a disaster area. "Kabed," Joryn asked with a grin as he entered, "have you been multi-tasking again?"

From behind a pile of unidentified parts to something-or-other, Kabed looked up to see the prince and answered with a sigh of intense determination, "You have no idea! Your father's got me upgrading everything all at once lately, not to mention the Unitrons he wants for all the soldiers. I've put together three so far. I keep telling him that I need some help. I mean, the pattern's set! If I just had more hands, I could build more of the things faster." He shook his head, frustrated and amused all at once.

It was no secret that Kabed never really minded being overworked. He loved to tinker and to build his machines. He was never truly content unless he was doing something with his hands.

"My father can be greedy." Joryn smiled. "We should never have told him you were a Deluvian tech wizard."

"Oh, I don't really mind the work. But going from swords and horses to light guns and robot unicorns is a tall order!

Deluvian science is so new to your father's empire, even after half a decade."

"And don't forget about *bionic* unicorns." Joryn laughed lightly.

"Ah, yes! A delay for which your father may *never* forgive me! But I'm quite proud of that particular accomplishment. And I'm pretty sure that Illium appreciates it."

"Oh, he does," Joryn answered. "He's the envy of all the unicorns in Nod that have ever been dismembered by giant crab monsters and lived to tell the tale."

Both men laughed at that.

"So, what brings you by, Joryn? Is it this mission to Chiroptera?"

"How do you know about that?"

Kabed shrugged. "Small empire. Word travels fast. Plus, I was adjusting the security cams in the throne room when it all went down."

"Ah," Joryn said. "I'll be sure and *not* tell my father you were eavesdropping."

"*He's* the one who wanted them adjusted right that minute, before you went to see him. But you're right. He'd probably still see it as eavesdropping. Likely try to kill me. Again. But enough of that. What is it that you need from me?"

"Well, we're fighting bat people. We're using stun rays only. No blood is to be shed, if at all possible, and no life is to be taken whatsoever. We are going in to get the harvest back, not to slaughter the Chirops."

"Yeah, I know. So," Kabed stood and went to the wall, taking down an odd looking, slender device that appeared to be a pair of wings and an engine of some sort attached to a harness, "I've got just the thing. This jetpack, or Aeropack, as I've taken to calling it, is easy to maneuver, fast, fuel efficient. I've made about ten of them."

"That's outstanding! But … I have to ask *why* you've made ten of them."

Another shrug. "Because it's easy, and I sometimes suffer from sleeplessness. I made the first one just because the idea came to me and one never knows when we're going to be attacked from the air again, like we were a few months ago. Dragons, as you are now surely aware, are not the only potential enemies with wings."

"Yes, you're a marvel, Kabed." Joryn considered. "Ten of them." He slapped Kabed on the shoulder with a wide grin. "Well, bring them along. I'll assign them to the warriors I feel should be in the air."

Kabed looked stunned. "*Along?* Bring them … *along?* I have plans tonight!"

"You have plans every night," Joryn pointed out. "And always with a different girl. Or one of your many projects. Just reschedule. There will be time enough for all of that *after* we've restored the harvest of the Highlands. Besides, I need you there, in case anything goes wrong with the light guns, or the jetpacks, or Illium." He laughed. "Don't look so sad! They have girls in both the Highlands *and* Chiroptera."

Kabed smiled. "That they do! I'll get packed. We're going by horseback, I assume? There aren't enough Unitrons to carry the whole company of troops you're taking in, and the few we have could outdistance the horses in very little time."

"Yes, and I'll be paired with Illium, who would much prefer to outrun the horses, but I'm sure he'll graciously slow his pace for the rest of you. And the Highland Elves have their own beasts."

"Klompers? I've never actually seen one before. Only pictures, but not up close. I've heard that they can run at twice the speed of a horse for short distances, even though they look much bulkier. Fascinating creatures." He considered. "It takes twelve hours by horseback to get to the Highlands from here. When are we leaving?"

"As soon as we're all prepared, unless King Orlok returns my father's call before the deadline, which is less than an hour from now. And unlikely. We should arrive there in time for a late dinner with their king. Of course, I'd much prefer it if Orlok would call and resolve the matter without soldiers."

Kabed nodded. "Very good. You know, when I left Deluvia, my greatest hope was that I would see the world in all its glorious diversity. Deluvia is so isolated, closed to outsiders as it is and, at present, submerged beneath the deadly waters of the sea. I wanted to see everything I'd heard was outside with my own eyes! It's ironic that I spend most of my time here, in this workshop. Rarely do I leave the king's city."

Joryn put a hand on his friend's shoulder. "Well, we're going to remedy that. There's much more to the diversity of Nod than the Royal City has to offer. Even I have seen very little of it. We're young, Kabed! We have so much time to see the best of the Empire. We should take full advantage of it."

"Agreed, but I'm not spending twelve hours on a horse. I'm taking one of the Unitrons. Promise I'll mind its pace."

Joryn smiled as he left. "Very well, Kabed. No one should feel neglected by your superior ride, since you did, after all, build the thing. I'll go and rally the troops. Meet us at the stables."

"I'm looking forward to it. Though … from what I've heard about Chiropteran women, I'm not sure *that* part of the journey is going to offer much motivation."

CHAPTER 3:
THE SAGA OF LIN SHIVVAN

ONCE THE SOLDIERS OF PALACE NOD, THE TRAVELERS from the Highlands, and Joryn's elite warriors were prepared, and the hour had passed without a word from King Orlok, the party set off on the twelve-hour journey to the Highlands of Imperial Nod. Joryn marveled at the elves' ability to sleep so peacefully, turned around on their klompers' shells. He imagined how the constant movement of the creatures' strides would have kept him from rest had he been on one of them. When Joryn grew tired on a journey, it had always been his way to make camp and let Illium rest as well. These elves were clearly used to having to make long journeys without pause, and the long-legged klompers were very much up to the task. Joryn worried over the horses of his soldiers as the journey wore on. They had to stop for water a number of times, but while the horses and Illium drank almost desperately from the streams and rivers when they stopped, the klompers seemed not the least bit interested.

Drae had explained to the prince that klompers could go a solid week without food or water, because they stored their excess food in the fatty deposits beneath their shells, and the shells themselves acted as both a cooling and a heating system that helped the animals manage the water in their bodies. The creatures, which were more or less eight-legged camels in tortoise shells, were suited to any number of environments, though they had been discovered specifically in the desert wastelands south of Palace Nod and imported to the Highlands seventy-nine years before Prince Joryn had been born. The creatures had quickly become the Highland Elves' most valued beasts of burden. Drae told Joryn how he had raised his own klomper, Shilo, from a calf when he himself had been only nine years old.

Joryn had patted Illium on the neck and, with a smile, told Drae that his unicorn steed had actually helped to raise *him* from the time he'd been born.

The group was welcomed late that night by Rune Ördo, the king of the Highland Elves. Their steeds were taken into luxurious stables, where they were bathed, watered, fed, and rested. All except for Illium, who preferred to remain with his friends. Even Kabed's Unitron was polished and treated like any other war steed on the eve of battle in the stables.

The rest of the group were treated to a great feast in the king's dining hall. There were dancers, and musicians, and laughter, and lighthearted conversation. This is how the elves always prepared for battle, with a night of revelry.

The evening's festivities wound down with the announcement of Anek'don, the storyteller. The music stopped. The dancers took seats on the floor rugs with the rest of the king's guests. The torches along the walls were largely doused, leaving enough light to see, but creating an ambiance of quiet anticipation.

Anek'don spoke: "Tonight, mighty warriors, in honor of Drae Shivvan, who has brought us the aid of our emperor, and in honor of Prince Joryn, the Peace-Bringer, and his courageous band, I shall deliver a tale that is most apropos. Tonight, I shall unfold for you the final part in *The Saga of Lin Shivvan*."

Shivvan. Joryn, who was seated right beside Drae Shivvan, looked to the warrior's countenance, and in the flickering light of the remaining torch fires, he saw the elf's features brace with stoicism, as if preparing for a blow from an enemy that could not be evaded. *Yes*, Joryn thought, *the name is no coincidence.* He looked back to the storyteller, eager to learn the significance of this tale to the elf that had brought his party to the Highlands.

"Lin Shivvan," the storyteller went on, "the younger brother of our great hero, Drae Shivvan, who sits among us this very night, was a great warrior in his own right. Lin Shivvan was the hero of the Battle of Moonstripe; he valiantly held off the great spiders of Taraqq-Norr with a single sword during the Great Siege, losing his noble klomper Seido to their poison in the process; he won the heart and hand of Lulanne, the daughter of the sorcerer Muaverellian, by his cleverness in unraveling the Riddle of Mount Strange, and with her he fathered his two sons, Jahbed and Tyro; but his greatest day, his most noble hour, was most certainly his last, when he stood by his brother in the battle that ended the war with the Chirops, half a decade ago, upon tomorrow's dawn.

"All of the Elves of the Highlands know the tale of how Chiroptera met us with enmity at every turn for generation after generation, seventy-six years in all. It was the battle of the Sea of Moss, where the mightiest warriors of both realms met in a final, bloody conflict. It is said that the green of the mosslands was fully painted over in red from the blood of the fallen that day. Chirops wasted no time in drinking as much as they could from each of their victims, before the next challenger called away their attention.

"It was during the final moments of this battle, when our great warrior, Lin Shivvan, breathed his last. He and his elder brother Drae had already killed hundreds of Chirop warriors that day with bow and arrow and sword.

"Mighty Lin, with the very sword he'd used to stave off the titanic spider horde, was locked in battle with Golrath, the greatest of the Chirop warriors, while beside him, his brother Drae battled another of Chiroptera's legends, Nightstorm the Merciless.

"It is no secret to any who have ever faced the Chirops in battle how difficult it is to fight them from the ground. One must be ever alert against being lifted into the sky by any Chiropteran other than the one before you, for this is the easiest way for the cowardly bat warriors to defeat us, by stealing us skyward when we least expect it and dropping us to our deaths.

"After an arduous duel, Lin at last knocked the sword from the hand of Golrath. Taking full advantage of his enemy's stunned countenance, Lin drove his legendary sword into the monster's heart, assuring the beast that was Golrath would never threaten the Highlands of Nod again.

"What Lin had not counted on was the wrath of Golrath's former student, Nightstorm. Upon his master's death, Nightstorm broke off his battle with Drae, leaping into the air and over the young warrior's head.

"Drae turned to meet him, expecting him to land behind him, but was too late in realizing that the villain had gone to the side and grabbed Lin instead.

"Still lost in the warmth of his victory, Lin had not been prepared for the attack. Nightstorm had grabbed him by the shoulders and wasted no time in lifting him up to the sky.

"Drae reached for his bow and tried to shoot Nightstorm out of the sky before he had climbed too far from the ground, but the cunning Chirop avoided every shot.

"When he was high enough to assure the drop would end the elf who had slain his master, Nightstorm let go, only to find that Lin had been prepared for the move, when the hero instantly took hold of the Chirop's wrist.

"Lin had dropped his sword upon being yanked into the air, but the dagger at his belt was equally capable of felling a foe at close range. He removed the dagger and made every attempt to sink it into his enemy's heart.

"Nightstorm tried to shake off the mighty elf, but found himself unable to do so. Both warriors were far too practiced.

"At last, Lin drew blood, slashing a shallow wound across the Chirop's face.

"Enraged even further, Nightstorm found new strength, gripping Lin's wrist and crushing it. Taking the dagger from Lin's useless hand, Nightstorm brutally stabbed him in the chest three times. With the third stab, he left the dagger in noble Lin's heart. He tore at the hero's throat with his fangs and glutted himself on heroic blood, before dropping the limp body of Lin Shivvan to break upon the moss-covered rocks of the battlefield.

"Drae, his heart breaking with sorrow at the loss of his brother, managed to strike the vile Chirop with an arrow to the shoulder.

"The creature's pain was such that he could no longer flap his mighty wings. He began to fall, but was caught by his fellows and flown away to be nursed back to health.

"Due to the heroic efforts of the brothers Shivvan, the Highland Elves declared victory at the Sea of Moss that day, and an end to the bloody conflict begun in the time of their grandfathers was at long last forced upon the people of Chiroptera. We have, until just yesterday, had no trouble from them since.

"This is the end of *The Saga of Lin Shivvan*, but one has to wonder, will a new chapter be written, should Drae Shivvan meet Nightstorm in battle once again? I can think of no more fitting an epilogue than the death of Nightstorm, at the hands of Lin's brother, and the long-awaited satisfaction of Clan Shivvan." The storyteller bowed and left the room in silence.

Joryn clapped his hands, once, before the restraining arm of Drae Shivvan stopped him. The warrior stared into the fire stoically, not turning to meet the questioning gaze of the young prince, as he whispered elucidation, "The greatest display of ovation, here in the Highlands, is total silence. Say nothing as we stand and depart from the great hall."

Joryn nodded silently, embarrassed, as he rose to his feet and followed the soundless crowd outside, though there was much he wanted to say. He now knew a great deal more about his new acquaintance, and he wondered if the suspicions of the priestess had been clarified for him in Anek'don's suggested epilogue to *The Saga of Lin Shivvan*.

CHAPTER 4:
PREPARATIONS FOR WAR

THAT NIGHT, JORYN, ILLIUM, AND KABED JOINED DRAE Shivvan, King Rune, and Rune's eldest son Prince Lothu in the king's war room to map out a strategy.

"I hate to say it, my prince," King Rune said to Joryn, "but the Chirops will *not* negotiate. We've had them as our enemies for too long not to anticipate them. They will meet your forces with bloodshed and nothing less."

"But surely, there must be some chance," Joryn protested, sounding as though he were pleading for another verdict.

"No," Drae said. "We must be prepared for combat the moment we cross into their territory."

Kabed interjected, "What sort of combat are we talking about exactly? What are their armaments? I'm from Deluvia, and I've not yet learned all there is to know about the kingdoms that lay outside the borders of the Empire. Though I have taken a little time to study the data we have on Chiropteran biology."

Prince Lothu answered him, "The Chirops will come at you with sword, axe, mace, and shield. They do not use bows and arrows, nor do they use these amazing light rays that your soldiers have brought. The light rays may prove the surprise that will be needed to gain the advantage on the battlefield. But they also have the high ground, no matter the field."

"Yes," Kabed agreed. "Their wings. We've got an answer for that, though I didn't have the time to equip all of our soldiers. I'll be training a few of the warriors of Nod and the Highlands to use mechanical flight packs. They'll be able to engage the Chirops in the air. I, myself, will be using this tech, as will Drae and Prince Joryn."

"And besides that," Joryn added, "the men and women we have on the ground will be well defended with their light guns. It sounds as though the Chirops have to get in close with their weapons in order to strike at all. Light guns can hit them long before they are in range to use their own weapons against us. They may have the higher ground, so to speak, but we have the greater technology, thanks to our friend Kabed. Victory should come easily."

Illium and the elves exchanged a look.

"My prince," Drae said carefully, "I advise caution. It is precisely when we think our victory is assured that the enemy will take us by surprise, using our overconfidence against us. I speak only as a seasoned warrior. I do not mean to argue."

"No," Joryn said with a warm smile. "Please, Drae, share your insights freely, and do not fear me for my father's sake. I confess that I am new at warfare, and I will bow to your wisdom on most matters."

"Save the killing, I suppose."

"Exactly," Joryn said in a manner both forceful and affable. "Which brings me to my next concern. Kabed, the light guns … If we use them on the Chirops in the air, even on stun, it occurs to me that fatalities may result from the fall. Perhaps we should instruct our warriors not to fire upon them until they are a survivable distance from the ground."

King Rune broke in, dismayed, "My prince, forgive me, but aren't we perhaps being too charitable? These are the fiends who robbed us of our crops, our livelihood, and we are discussing in my *war* room how to keep them from being injured when we shoot them out of the sky? I don't see how that will do anything but complicate matters."

"We will not take one single life, Your Majesty," Joryn affirmed. "All life is sacred, even the lives of our enemies."

King Rune looked as though he were about to unleash a tirade against this, when Kabed broke in deftly, "My lords, this is actually a non-issue. As I said, I've done some reading up on Chirop biology. I can assure you that when we hit them with our stun rays, no matter how high off the ground they are, they will survive the fall. They have an involuntary reaction to going unconscious during flight which probably helped their ancestors survive long journeys." He looked to Joryn with a reassuring smile. "Their wings will save them, my prince. They are in no danger once they are stunned."

Joryn nodded, relieved that he would no longer have to defend his position to the king of the Highlands. "That's good to know, Kabed. Thank you for your research." He looked to the others. "So we can hit the Chirops wherever they are. We should be able to overpower them," he looked to Drae, "but we should also beware of overconfidence, as you said. What are their numbers?"

"Unimaginable," Prince Lothu answered. "You're going to the place where they *all* live, and they're a warrior culture. Very few of them will *not* be flying out of the mountain with swords when you arrive."

"Yes," Drae added. "I'd anticipate thousands. We *will* be outnumbered. There is no getting around that. But Joryn is right that we do have the more advanced weaponry. Our chances are good for victory, otherwise I would not be supporting this effort."

"When the Chirops surrender—," Joryn began, but was cut off by the laughter of the elves. "Have I missed something," he asked.

"The Chirops never surrender," Drae explained. "It's a matter of honor among their warriors. To surrender is shameful. That's why we normally just *kill* them, my prince. And when they are forced to retreat, they usually retreat back to the very mountain we are shortly invading. They will have nowhere to run. We will have to stun every last Chirop warrior if we are to win the day."

Joryn nodded, understanding. He looked to Illium, who offered him a reassuring nod.

The unicorn had yet to decide whether or not he cared to speak to the elves, and so he listened intently as the discussion went on.

Joryn pressed onward. "Your Majesty, I know my ways are not your own. That being said, I *will* succeed in restoring to your people what is yours, and my methods will be unlikely to give you any confidence now, but I give you my word."

"My prince," the king replied, "your wisdom is renowned throughout the Empire and beyond. You are the Peace-Bringer, and I have every confidence that your ways can win the day just as well as our own. Forgive me for simply not being able to hide my surprise at your methods."

"Thank you, King Rune." Joryn looked around the group. "We will hit them hard the moment we cross the border, if they attack as you anticipate. If they do not, we will ask for parley with King Orlok, which I suspect, from your accounts, will not be granted, at which point we start shooting anyway.

"During the battle, I will make my way to the mountain to try to gain entry. If the Chirops do not surrender, then we *must* get to King Orlok in order to force our terms. Leave the negotiation to me. I think I can work around his honor issues. I'm sure of it."

"If you are captured," the king warned, "they will keep you alive. You will become a powerful bargaining chip. They will not be as merciful to your warriors, however. You may hold the lives of your enemies as sacred, my prince, but I assure you the Chirops do not see things the same way."

"Perhaps after tomorrow, King Rune, they will." Joryn smiled confidently, though he felt it was a dishonest presentation at best. He doubted himself terribly but knew better than to let it show. "And the fact that I'd make such an enticing captive may help keep me alive all the way to the king's chamber, at the heart of the mountain."

"I'll accompany you," Drae put in, placing a hand on the young man's shoulder. "We will enter the caverns of the mountain together."

Joryn nodded at him, grateful.

"This plan is crazy," King Rune said with a weary shake of his head. "I'll just wait with bated breath for word of your victory. I cannot risk the life of my heir to this suicide mission of yours, even though I am equally certain that your chances are good as I am that you are walking into a bloodbath." He looked to Joryn. "You are, after all, the same prince who, when his palace was under siege by the dragons, simply said, 'I'll talk to them,' and succeeded in brokering the most *impossible* peace! Why should I doubt that you will do the very same in Chiroptera, with an army at your back, as you did in Din, with nothing but the Sword of Libran and a unicorn?"

"Well," Kabed put in, patting Illium's iron shoulder, "he is quite a unicorn, sire."

The king laughed, meeting Illium's eyes and taking in the marvel that was his bionic body. "He is indeed." He looked to the others. "And now, we must retire. Dawn brings war, and you must all be well rested and well fed before you leave."

Everyone bowed their heads as the king and his eldest son left the room. When they had gone, the warriors each went their separate ways to prepare what needed preparing and then to sleep.

Once he'd dressed for bed, Joryn found Illium and confided in his oldest friend, "I'm scared, Illium. I have nowhere near the confidence I was showing in there with the king. These warriors know better than I how to wage war. How will I ever gain the confidence I need to lead the way that everyone thinks I should be able to do. I feel cursed by my victory with the dragons."

Illium winked. "Present your confidence to those who follow you, then grow into it. It's as simple as that."

Joryn laughed and stroked Illium's mane affectionately. "Everything's always so simple with you." He hugged the unicorn around the neck. "And you're usually right."

"I'm always right," Illium corrected; a smile in his voice.

Joryn laughed again. "That you are. Sleep well, my friend." With that, Joryn went to his bed and deliberated over the battle to come in his imagination, with forced confidence, until he fell asleep, at which point he continued the process in his dreams, unable to escape the dread conflict even in his slumber.

The following morning, before the sun had risen, three members of the royal family met in the sprawling garden under cover of dark.

Princess Hero and her younger brother Prince Vail approached the waiting figure of Princess Maressah, all of them adorned in dark cloaks to further hide their movements.

"Were you seen by anyone?" Maressah asked them.

"Not that we could tell," Vail answered.

Hero studied the urgent look on her sister-in-law's face. The request for a pre-dawn, clandestine meeting had come just after evening meal, with no explanation as to the need of it aside from that very same look, which Maressah must have been wearing throughout the night.

"I'd ask if everything is all right," Hero offered, "but I'm not a fool. So, I'll just get to it and ask what the secret is."

Maressah nodded, smiling tightly. "Thank you both for meeting me here. I must speak to you about the mission the emperor has given to Joryn. I am deeply concerned. The only secret is that I have uttered a word on the matter that might be seen to defy the emperor's will."

Hero offered a subtle grin in silent approval. She liked Maressah. Everyone did it seemed. But Hero didn't like her for her heritage as the daughter of King Willfriez of the kingdom of Aise, or for her regal demeanor and perfect posture, or even for her staggering beauty, all of which made Maressah the ideal wife for the crown prince of the Empire. No, Hero liked Maressah for what lay beneath the surface; the cunning, the heart of gold, the daring spirit that never ignored an opportunity to confront an injustice. Kail's heart had served him well when he'd fallen in love with her. The royal siblings may have still jokingly referred to Maressah as 'the *new* princess,' but Hero had long since accepted her into the family. "Rest assured, this conversation will remain between us."

Vail sneered. "We are no strangers to our father's ... less admirable qualities."

"Even so," Maressah continued, "what I am going to say is dangerous. What I am going to suggest would no doubt enrage your father to actions I dare not imagine. But I fear he has sent your youngest brother on a mission from which he is not expected to return."

Hero and Vail nodded in silent agreement, eager to hear what Maressah was getting at.

"Joryn is very dear to my husband," Maressah continued. "And he's very dear to me. If he is killed at the head of the army, as I fear the emperor hopes, I cannot imagine the consequences to our hearts or to our relationship with your father. Besides that, it is simply wrong." She shook her head, angrily, though she kept her tone even and her tenor calm. "To send someone with no experience whatsoever in leading armies on such a mission; to spit such venom at Joryn over the past weeks. The emperor fears him, and now he has the means to see him removed. I have no doubt of his intentions." She met the eyes of the brother and sister before her. "And I want the two of you to help your brother come through the battle alive."

Vail stood tall, grinning from ear to ear. "We shall leave at once! No Chirop will ever get near to—" His sister's hand landing across his chest silenced him, and he looked to her, questioning.

"Calm down, Little Brother. Think for once before you speak." To Maressah, she said, "Not that I'm all that hesitant to agree with him, but why us?"

Maressah smiled. "Because, it would not do for the wife of the crown prince to sneak away in the night in clear defiance of an Imperial command. For me to go would be seen as irrefutably subversive."

"So why not ask any of the others?" Hero asked.

"I may have only been a part of this family for a little over a year," Maressah answered, "but I feel that I have come to know my eleven new brothers and sisters well. There are others I might trust, yes. But I cannot ask *all* of you to go. That would be too conspicuous. As for you two in particular, not only do I trust you, but you seem to have a knack for getting both into and *out* of trouble. And you're no strangers to warfare. More than simply trusting you to go, to see that Joryn is not overwhelmed by this command that has been forced upon him, I trust you to return alive yourselves when the task is done."

"Okay, Vail, carry on," Hero said.

"As I was saying," he beamed, "you will have our swords, and so will Joryn."

"The issue is that it is a twelve-hour ride to the Highlands. Another hour to Chiroptera. How could we possibly get there before the battle begins?" Hero was not doubting as much as she was thinking aloud, searching her mind for a solution.

"Which is why I asked you to meet me so early," Maressah said. "Far be it from me to send you on any criminal errands, of course, but it is said that unicorns can travel twice the distance of a horse in the same amount of time." She nodded to herself, feigning innocence. "I have often heard Kabed bragging that his Unitrons can outpace even a natural unicorn, and that they have no need for rest."

Vail grinned mischievously, looking to Hero. "Remember the time you broke into—?"

"Way ahead of you." Hero chuckled. "Kabed's workshop won't keep us out for long."

***

Joryn awoke with the sun, surprised to feel rested and ready for the day ahead. He and Drae Shivvan set to work immediately preparing their warriors for the journey to Chiroptera and the battle to follow. Joryn noticed the sneers on the faces of several of the elves, as Drae confirmed the rumors they had heard, that there was to be no bloodshed, by order of the prince of Nod. He knew they thought him a fool, and maybe he was, but he had made the decision he thought he could live with, and he was going to stand by it. The people of Nod had shed each other's blood for too long. There were better ways to settle a conflict. He had shown them so in Din, and he hoped to show them again on this very day.

The elves loaded their klompers with weapons and supplies. The soldiers of Nod mounted their horses. Joryn found his "elite," as they had come to be known, clustered together. He approached them and climbed onto Illium's back, patting the unicorn on the neck affectionately. "I know we can do this," he said to them. "But I need your help." Without realizing it, he looked questioningly at Onri Sprigg. "We have to lead by example, show them we're not afraid to face the enemy with peace as our ultimate goal, rather than destruction. What say you?"

Onri spoke up eagerly, "I say that yours *is* the better way. We will overcome the enemy, and all of them will live to tell the tale of our victory."

"Yes, they will." Joryn smiled at the Lowland Elf. "I trust Kabed explained the workings of the Aeropacks to all of you this morning."

Kabed answered proudly, "You, me, Onri, Drae, three soldiers of Nod, and three warriors of the Highlands have been trained to use them, and all show exceptional skill."

Quickwing laughed. "That's because your toys are easy to play with, Kabed." He unfurled his great white wings, as he stretched his arms and yawned. "I prefer the real thing myself."

Joryn rolled his eyes with a smirk. "Modest as ever, Quickwing. So are we ready to march on the mountain?"

The group nodded solemnly.

Again, he looked pointedly at Onri. "Then let us ride together to the front line and lead the way to Chiroptera and a peaceful resolution."

With that, the elite warriors of Nod met Drae at the front of the battle group, and the hour's journey to the realm of the bat people was under way at last.

The wall screen in King Orlok's throne room lit up at his command, replaying the message he'd received from a spy in the Highlands one more time.

The image of a Chirop in a hooded robe appeared on the screen. His wings were concealed beneath the robe in a way that would have made him appear, from a distance, as though he were an elf with a severely disfigured spine. His face hidden in shadow, the spy spoke in a hushed tone, looking behind him periodically as he made his report. "My king, I have news from the Highlands. King Rune has secured the aid of Emperor Sapros in taking back the Highland crops. An army is setting out from the Highlands within the hour, led by Drae Shivvan and Libran's supposed champion, Prince Joryn of the Imperial capital. They are leaving on klompers and horseback. They will be no match for you once they arrive.

"Their only advantage would have been surprise, which I'm undoing for them now. It's half a day's ride from here on the horses, if they stop at intervals to let the animals rest, as I'm sure they will. This Imperial prince they have brought in has a heart for every form of life; a fatal weakness.

"I would have sent word sooner, but it is very difficult to conceal my presence among the elves, as you know, and I wanted to get closer to learn the nature of the aid Sapros had sent before reporting in. I hope this message is of service." With a final backward turn of his head, the spy on the screen reached for the control on his end and broke off the transmission.

"Well?" the king asked the general he had invited to his chambers to view the spy's transmission.

"Drae Shivvan," rumbled the harsh voice of the general, Nightstorm the Merciless, as he reached to his face and caressed the scar that he'd earned years before. "His brother gave me this, after killing my mentor."

"Yes," said King Orlok, "and you repaid him for it by piercing his heart. But you know the power of a vengeful spirit, Nightstorm. If Drae is leading this attack, he will be blinded by it. He will want to target you above all else. Use this to your advantage."

Nightstorm grinned hungrily. "Indeed." He looked to the king with a sobering thought. "Drae Shivvan is as nothing to me, but his companions may prove more dangerous. This prince of Nod, the supposed champion of Libran … did he not face down the dragons, alone? Now he has an army at his command."

The king croaked out a hateful laugh. "Legends are always disproportionate to the truth, Nightstorm. I am certain money changed hands in vast amounts to broker the peace with the dragons. Just as I am certain the true Sword and Shield of Libran *remain* lost, if they ever existed at all. This prince is a fraud, the pawn of his father, nothing more. Do not fear him or the power of his *myth*."

Nightstorm nodded. "Yes, Your Majesty."

"All that mythology aside, what are your thoughts on our defense against this meager force?"

"We will overpower them quickly and easily, my king. We will have nowhere to retreat or regroup but Mount Chirop itself, so I will see to it that we have no such need. The humans have never faced us in battle and, no matter what they have been told by their allies from the Highland kingdom, they will be unprepared. It will be just like fighting the elves."

The king growled. "The last time we fought with the elves, a treaty was forced by their prowess on the battlefield."

"Yes," agreed Nightstorm casually. "However, they have had half a decade to grow soft and forgetful. They were not prepared for the strike you ordered on their crops. They offered only the weakest resistance, and now they've had barely a day to prepare for a counter offensive.

"I will take out all of our warriors and meet this army the moment they cross our border. We will overwhelm them and feast on their blood.

"No further battle group will dare enter the territory of the Chirops any time soon, after the rain of blood that will greet these fool humans and elves who dare to resist us."

"Good," King Orlok said with satisfaction. "Now, go and prepare our warriors. Not one of the enemy's number should be left alive. We will feast on their blood, as you have promised, and the kingdoms of the *Empire* will at last learn to fear the outlying kingdoms, as I let them watch me dine on the blood of their favorite son."

"It will be done, my king." Nightstorm turned and left the room, eager for the bloody feast of battle to come and looking forward to sending Drae Shivvan to join his brother in Merigo, the unreachable land of the dead in the distant west.

CHAPTER 5:
THE WORKINGS OF LIBRAN

TIANNA SAT ALONE, HER BACK TO THE ALTAR IN THE Temple of Libran, over which she was the chosen guardian. The nagging feeling that something was not right about Drae Shivvan had left her restless all night, as she'd struggled to sleep.

Tianna had just returned from a walk in the courtyard, where she had addressed the concerns of Prince Kail's wife, Maressah. The princess had been less than pleased at the king's treatment of her husband's youngest brother. In response, she had offered borderline rebellious advice to another prince and princess of the palace; advice that she hoped would give Joryn some unexpected aid from his family. Tianna had agreed with Maressah's actions and had offered her support. Now that she had returned to the temple, however, she decided to give the matter of Drae Shivvan her full attention.

Few people ever visited the Temple of Libran that stood on the grounds of Palace Nod, for few people ever considered that asking for help from the god of balance could actually aid them in all things. They preferred to go to the temples of the gods of war, or fertility and wealth, thinking success in these matters was paramount and would make them happy. Tianna felt blessed to have been chosen as one of Libran's priestesses in her infancy. Learning the ways of balance seemed to her a much more peaceful existence than what the other priests and priestesses had been condemned to.

She knew nothing of her parents or where she had been born. She knew only that she had been recognized for certain gifts that were valued in a priestess. Before being appointed to the temple at Palace Nod, she had been trained to use these abilities, to prophesy for the odd citizen who sought the wisdom of her god, to see what could not be seen, to hear what could not be heard.

Tianna sat cross-legged on the floor, back straight, eyes closed, and she cleared her mind of all but Drae Shivvan. The Highland Elf had been sincere. The bat folk had attacked and pillaged his people's crops. The plea for the emperor's help in the matter was genuine. But what was it that he was hiding? What was it that had troubled her psychic subconscious so unrelentingly?

She decided that she could do with another examination of the warrior. She focused on his presence, tracking it from Palace Nod to wherever he had journeyed by now. Her powerful mind's eye covered the ground more quickly than any steed or air ship could travel, catching the pungent scent of the klompers and horses, following their path to the Highlands, and at last locating the group of soldiers very near the mountainous territory of Chiroptera.

She found him.

Drae was seated on his loyal klomper's shell, as the creature trotted at a steady pace ahead of the others, alongside Joryn and Illium. She felt the elf's frustration at having to keep pace with the much slower horses, wishing there had been enough klompers to spare, or that more of them had been on the mechanical Unitrons that Kabed had invented. She probed deeper into his feelings, hoping for a clue as to what he was hiding. She could not read his thoughts outright. That gift was beyond her. She could feel what he felt though, very plainly.

As the elf looked to Prince Joryn, riding beside him, she felt a great ocean of conflicted emotions in him. That struck her as odd. The elf seemed to both admire and detest the young prince. She noted that the admiration seemed centered around the young man's posture, his strength of character and commitment to his morals, while the loathing came from the recognition that Joryn was uncomfortable with command, with war, with violence of any kind. The elf found the young prince insufferably naïve, as did the other warriors from the Highlands … but that was getting her off task. She made herself focus on Drae.

What was it?

Guilt was the overwhelming emotion as Drae studied the prince. Guilt? What was the elf getting them into? Was it a trap? Deeper she probed, finding Drae's pain, his anger, his sense of loss, of bloodlust. He wanted revenge, but for what? And how did that contribute to his guilty feelings over Prince Joryn? Was he going to betray him? Was there to be bloodshed in spite of the prince's command?

The Highland Elf looked ahead again, to the mountains of Chiroptera which they were fast approaching. He seemed to settle on something. His resolve was strengthened. He rubbed his arm, and then she saw it: the glowing symbol of Centaurus, the god of war.

Tianna opened her eyes with a gasp. "He's made a deal with a god!" *But what?* she thought. *What does it matter? Do not all warriors ask the gods for victory before entering a conflict?* She wanted to dismiss it. She wanted it to be nothing, but how could she? Alerting her friends to the feelings she had gotten off of Drae, along with the commitment he had to the war god could … what? Save the day? Defeat the elf's plot to betray the prince? Probably not. Most likely, her concerns would be dismissed, because the facts were not substantial in themselves. She had no proof that anything was truly out of the ordinary or in any way a threat to the mission. She let her shoulders drop, and she sighed with resignation.

"Why so quick to give up, my child?"

She turned with a start, and she clumsily got to her feet at the unexpected sound of the voice behind her, and then just as quickly fell back to the ground, prostrating herself before the mighty visitor. "Libran! My lord! My god!"

The gentle voice demurred, "Please stand, Priestess, and do not worship me. I have never myself claimed to be a god, though Libran I am."

She stood, awed. Even for those committed to the temple life, physical visits from the very gods they served were rare to the point of being almost unheard of. "If ... If you are not a god ... then what ...?"

He smiled, and it was contagious. "Just a friend. A messenger, who would see this world in balance. I have chosen a champion to that end, and his safety is greatly important to me. No harm must come to him, and to *that* end, I have also chosen you, to help protect him."

"But ... if I may ask?"

"You may ask me anything, Tianna." The being smiled with his whole presence, as he gazed lovingly down at her smaller form.

"You are so powerful! If not a god, then a being far beyond us. You went to Joryn, as he said, helping him to save Illium in the Broken Desert, you gave him your sword and shied. Why do you need me at all?"

"Because, to put it very honestly, this is not my world. I intervened in the desert, because the intervention of the other so-called gods of Nod against Joryn required me to balance their efforts with my own. But I did not fight the alleged demigod Warclaw *for* the prince. I went to him when he surrendered to the Higher Power. It would not serve Nod, were I to intervene personally at every dark turn. You, the people of Nod who love peace, must face these conflicts on your own, if they are ultimately to be eliminated. And it will take time, perhaps generations, before Nod can be truly and finally at peace. Joryn will need to know that he has *your* friendship, and the friendship of his followers, of Kabed and Illium, of his brothers and sisters, far more than he needs any further assurances from me. This is *your* world, and all of you must play your part to win it accordingly. I will guide you, when it is necessary. I will step in when the balance demands that I do so. But for the most part, I will not intervene."

"Then why intervene now? Why come to me and say these things, rather than letting me come to these conclusions on my own?"

"Because, my child, there isn't time, and I am not the only so-called god who has done so in this matter."

"Centaurus!"

Libran nodded. "And so the balance required my further intervention. For the rest, I suggest you ask Centaurus himself."

"Through his priests?"

Libran smiled, an amused and knowing look in his eyes. "Would you trust them more than yourself?" He stepped forward and brushed her hair back gently with his fingers. "You have many gifts that you have not allowed yourself to embrace, for fear that your spiritual instincts are lying to you. The powers you *feel* at your command are more than any other priest or priestess has ever had. If you trust your own instincts about Drae Shivvan, then why do you not trust these other intuitions as well?"

The light of revelation came on in the young priestess' eyes. "I could command him here. I could bind him here and demand answers to my suspicions." In a whisper she added, "I know how to do it. I have dreamt it many times."

Libran startled her then, as she felt his pride wash over her like a tidal wave of warmth in her spirit. "I have been watching you since you were born, my child. You were even then meant to be my priestess here and now. Trust in yourself and in your friends. You will be faced with many dangers throughout your life. You will see mighty victories and suffer terrible losses. But you will always have friends who love you. And you will always have *my* love. I leave you with this token of my own devotion." He stepped aside and revealed a shining, metallic eagle that was perched on the altar.

"It's beautiful," Tianna breathed.

"Thank you, Priestess," said the eagle, in a smooth, masculine voice.

Tianna started, then looked to Libran. "It speaks!"

Libran laughed lightly. "Indeed he does. Perhaps too much." He raised a glowing eyebrow at the bird.

"I know when to keep my beak shut, Libran," the eagle assured him. "You know me." The metallic wings of the creature adjusted, and it composed itself, sitting taller than before, as if full of pride.

"That I do. And all too well," Libran answered affectionately. He looked to the priestess. "Allow me to introduce my dear friend Iron Bill."

"Hello," Tianna offered uncertainly to the bird.

"At your service, Priestess," the eagle spoke with unmistakable confidence.

"I have given my champion a sword and shield," Libran explained to Tianna. "The least I can give ..." he paused and studied her with as much wonder in his eyes as she had felt upon studying him.

She could feel it radiating off of him. Suddenly she knew him for the being that he was. Not a god, but a friend and guardian. A being with only the best in mind for the people of Nod.

"The least I can give my devoted priestess is this true companion and messenger. Iron Bill is the last of his kind. There were so many once, in Deluvia, where they were created, but they became something of a threat to a corrupt ruler long, long ago."

Tianna noticed the lowering of the eagle's head, and she felt sorrow—suppressed, old, but still very strong—emanating from him. "He's alive!" She looked to Libran, then, feeling rude, turned to the bird himself. "You're alive!"

"Well, that's good to know," said Iron Bill. "Residing as long as I have above the clouds on the Mountain of the Twelve, I was beginning to wonder. Now when can I see some action? It's been too long, and I yearn for the thrill of adventures again." He stretched out his wings as if testing his strength and laughed to himself as he winked at his new friend.

"Yes, he's very much alive," Libran added. "And his heart is brave and true."

Bill's chest puffed out at this, and he folded his wings neatly behind him.

"Iron Bill can travel at near the speed of light, making him the perfect messenger when needed. He is also armed with a powerful form of ancient Deluvian light weaponry that is now banned in that realm and has been for centuries. He has seen many things and can offer sound counsel. Trust him as you would trust me. As I shall not come to you in person except when necessary, he will be a reminder to you that I am with you always in spirit and in heart, my priestess."

Libran reached out a warmly glowing hand and caressed her cheek unexpectedly. "My Tianna." He offered her one last parting smile. "And now I must go. There are still others whom I intend to bring to Joryn's side this day."

With that, Libran walked the main aisle from the altar, just as any other man would, and stepped outside of the temple and into the sunlight, where Tianna watched, as he unfurled his magnificent glowing wings and lifted off as effortlessly as though he were simply floating into the air.

Tianna turned, looked to the metal eagle seated on the altar, and said to herself, "That just happened." She remembered herself. "I know what to do."

CHAPTER 6:
ARRIVAL AT THE CHIROPTERAN BORDER

A T THE ROCKY BORDER OF CHIROPTERA, ACROSS WHICH the sky was actually darker, full of clouds as it was, Joryn called the soldiers of Nod and the Highlands to a halt from Illium's back. He spoke loudly and clearly, so that all could hear. "We stand at the border of our enemy. I want to take this moment to assure you one last time of the justness of our cause and of our victory to come."

"We'll have victory in Merigo, after the Chirops kill us!" an angry voice spat from the ranks of the Highland Elves. "How are we supposed to defeat *flying* warriors without killing them? It can't be done!"

Joryn stared the elf down stoically, trying to hide how deeply the words had wounded his already shaky confidence.

An all too familiar voice defended the prince, "Mind your tongue, or I'll tear it out of your mouth and shove it up your stinky doo hole, *Highlander!*"

"Onri," Joryn broke in, "your loyalty is noted, but all of these warriors have a right to follow their hearts."

"Follow them into the grave you mean?" the angry elf pushed on.

Others of his kind chimed in as well then, murmuring their agreement.

"Ton La! Stop this!" Drae Shivvan was genuinely ashamed of his warriors' behavior. "You will obey your superiors without *question*. We are headed into battle and can have no dissention."

"We *will* obey our superior, Shivvan, and that man is *you*, not this green, idealistic pacifist!" Ton La replied. "We will *not* obey him, especially when he commands us not to take lives in a *battle*, and to use these blasted Deluvian light guns set for *stun*! He's marching us to our deaths! All of the Highlands will be filled with weeping widows and orphans this day, and the thought of our heroic ghosts will do little to comfort them!"

"Ton La! All of you," Drae retorted. "*I* am commanding you to follow these directives. We will ride into Chiroptera with our light guns set to stun. We will take no life, and we *will* follow the commands of the *emperor's son*! The next one of you to open his or her mouth in dissent will have volunteered to be the first to fall at my light gun's stun beam!" He noted their shamed silence, then nodded to Joryn.

"As I was saying," the prince continued, "you all have a right to follow your hearts. If you feel that there is no honor in following me and my commands, then turn back now, and I will say nothing. For now, we ride, into Chiroptera!"

The men and women of Nod cheered, and the elves of the Highlands remained silent. Joryn wondered if this was the same silence that served as applause for their people, or if it was in itself a loud statement of no confidence in his right to lead them. Illium trotted forward, with Joryn on his back, and Joryn sighed loudly, releasing his great stress, as the warriors from the capital followed on their steeds.

Drae's klomper Shilo trotted close to Illium, and Drae spoke his mind, "You are new at this."

"Yes," Joryn answered, noting in silence that the Highland warriors had only resumed riding after Drae had urged his klomper forward. "I would much rather have relied upon diplomacy, to be honest. Your men and women ... they don't trust me. It's going to get them killed. We can't have division in our ranks before we even engage our enemy."

Drae nodded. "You seem to learn quickly, my prince. They will follow you. They are seasoned warriors and know that they must respect the chain of command."

"But they also know that I'm 'green,' " Joryn countered. "I'm 'idealistic,' and that's true. I am. My idealism has served me well thus far."

"Yes," Drae conceded, "with the dragon queen. My warriors know this. You may be new to overseeing international conflicts, but you have already accomplished the unthinkable with your tactics. Ton La is a blowhard. I will see to him, if he speaks out against you again."

Joryn took in the sight of the noble elf champion who rode beside him. He felt both intimidated and proud to be riding into this conflict at the side of such a seasoned hero as Drae Shivvan. He thought of the previous night's conclusion to *The Saga of Lin Shivvan* and was struck by a particular fact. "I am surprised to see you with a sword at your side, rather than the bow that you are famous for."

Drae smiled somberly. "It is the sword of my brother Lin. The very sword he dropped during his final battle with Nightstorm. I thought it only fitting that I carry it with me into Chiroptera. Perhaps it's sentimental, but I feel as if I am traveling with Lin at my side by carrying his sword. Wherever I take it, I believe his spirit is surely with me." *And I will use this very sword to exact my revenge on the one who took his life.*

He noticed, by the prince's thoughtful nod, that the young man respected the sentiment. After all, Joryn had *many* brothers and sisters who surely meant as much to him as Lin had to Drae. "I'm going to give it to his eldest son one day; my nephew Jahbed, when he's old enough."

"Drae Shivvan," Joryn asked, "may I call you my friend?"

Drae considered that. Though he did not understand the young human, he found himself liking him. The boy was unsure of himself, but he wasn't letting it show to anyone but his second in this mission. He had an inner strength and courage that trumped his personal fears. Under ordinary circumstances, Drae would have been glad to take the prince's hand in friendship. Under ordinary circumstances, he would also not have lied to his warriors about obeying Joryn's commands, for he himself was pledged to take at least two lives in the course of the coming battle, and no amount of friendly offers would rob him of his revenge.

Just as he began to truly like the prince, he began to loathe himself in equal degree, but it did nothing to change his mind. The deed must be done. And he *would* succeed. He had the power of his god Centaurus behind him.

Of course, he realized, as he eyed the sword and shield at Joryn's side, the prince also had the backing of a god. Perhaps killing him was not as easily guaranteed as he had convinced himself it would be.

Still, the boy's lack of experience in combat would surely work against him. He hadn't been forced to defend himself in open combat with stun guns in the land of the dragons after all. The Chirops might kill him quickly, and then Drae's hands would be clean; aside from the fact that he had arranged the entire conflict.

At last he answered, "You may, my prince." It was getting easier to lie the more often he did it.

"Then, in confidence," Joryn replied, "I am asking you to handle not just Ton La, but all of the Highland Elves. If I do not command them directly, they will have no opportunity to undermine me, and I know that you will not so undermine me." He looked earnestly into the elf's eyes. "You have my trust and my friendship, Drae Shivvan. Lead your warriors as I would, and we *will* have victory. I promise you."

Drae nodded his acquiescence and fell back to contemplate the battle now so near at hand.

Joryn, too, fell to silent contemplation and dread.

"Fear not, my prince," Illium offered. "You are doing well with the warriors at your command."

"Thank you, Illium. I would love to have your confidence." He patted the bionic unicorn gently on the neck.

"Listen to Illium, lump head," a female voice chimed in.

Joryn turned to his left to see two cloaked figures catching up to Illium on Unitrons.

The one who had spoken removed her hood and smiled at him with absolute self-assuredness.

"Hero? Is it really you?" Joryn was elated.

"Of course, Little Brother." The princess patted the broad-sword at her side. "And how dare you sneak away and keep all the fun to yourself?"

Joryn laughed. "I'd hardly call it 'sneaking away' when Father ordered me to lead his army into Chiroptera." He eyed his sister's sword. "No killing, by the way."

"Yeah, I heard something about that. Fortunately for you, the offspring of Lady Leita love a challenge."

She looked to the rider beside her. "Take down your hood already, twerp! There's no more reason to conceal our identities. We're at the front line now."

The young man did as requested. "Good! I loathe hiding! Let's stun the hell out of these sinister bat folk!" He added more quietly to Joryn, "Though, I would still like to draw my sword at some point. You know, just for effect."

"Ever the melodramatic one, Vail," Joryn said warmly. "Do as you like, as long as no one dies. *Including* yourself." He took the sight of his half-siblings in, the daughter and son of his father's fourth wife, Lady Leita. "You can't possibly know how good it is to have you both here at my side. My assurance has tripled just in the past few seconds. But how …?"

"Well," Hero offered, "Maressah suggested you might need some help, even though our father, we knew, would never allow it. So, we borrowed Kabed's Unitrons and rushed here at full speed."

"We stole them," Vail corrected.

"Borrowed," Hero insisted.

"Forgive me, sister," Vail went on, "if I ignore the fact that hacking into Kabed's computerized lock and then cutting through the Unitrons' restraints with our swords is *obviously* only borrowing, but saying we stole them sounds more daring."

"Well," Joryn put in, "either way, I am *very* glad to have you both here."

"Yes," Vail said. "We think that Father means for you to be killed on the battlefield. We are not here for the mission, brother, but to see you home alive."

"Yes," Hero agreed. "*Our* mission."

Joryn was deeply moved by the gesture, loving his sister and brother all the more for it, but he could not give way to the tide of emotion that had begun to bring tears to his eyes. He could not look vulnerable in front of the Highlanders who already thought him too weak for the task at hand. He blinked back the tears and nodded. "Thank you. Both of you. Your experience in combat will be needed here. I have not the history to lead warriors into battle. Truth to tell, I've only ever fought against another for my life twice. I'm no warrior."

"Right," Hero said sarcastically. "You only ever fought for your life twice … against a *demigod!* Who the hell are you to show anyone how to fight indeed?" She laughed and slapped him on the shoulder affectionately.

"But I lost." He looked to Illium's bionic shoulders, recalling the horrific reason for their existence.

"But you lived," Hero assured him with a confident wink.

"Hey!" Kabed's voice shouted indignantly from a little ways behind, where he had been chatting up one of the female warriors from the Highlands. "Are those my Unitrons?"

CHAPTER 7:
THE POWER OF THE PRIESTESS

"**T**HIS IS INTERESTING," IRON BILL OBSERVED CASUAL-ly, still seated upon the altar.

Tianna finished laying her circle of stones on the floor, standing back and wondering at the size. "I just hope it's big enough. I've only ever met one god ... I mean ... uh ... whatever they are ... things." She shrugged the magnitude of her theological disillusionment away with a shake of her head.

"Libran prefers the term 'Guardian,' if you really want to know," the bird offered. "It's what they all once were."

Tianna considered. "Guardian. That works."

"So, what exactly is all this?" Bill nodded towards her circle of rocks.

"I'm going to bind Centaurus here."

"In a circle of rocks?" He struggled not to add *Are you completely mad?* to his exclamation. He knew she needed to have faith in herself, and, frankly, he needed to believe in her too if that were ever to occur. "You're the priestess," he added instead.

"I know how to do this. I've seen it before in my dreams."

"You dream about binding Guardians with rocks?" He shook his head. "Poor girl. I shall endeavor to find you a mate the moment this ordeal is behind us."

She laughed shortly. "Priestesses don't have 'mates,' Bill."

The bird shook his head mournfully. "Neither do last-of-their kind metallic birds. Forgive me, Priestess."

"No harm done, old bird. For now, the dreams I *have* had will suffice to save my friends." She sat cross legged on the floor once more, closed her eyes, then thought better of it. She stood, mentally calling upon all of the power she had always secretly felt that she had. She spoke with a strength her voice had never known, an authority none could deny. "Centaurus, *Guardian* of war! I, the priestess Tianna, summon you! Stand now before me."

A light appeared, floating within the circle of stones at eye level to Tianna.

Iron Bill flew from the altar and perched in the rafters.

Only laughter emanated from the light; a condescending laughter at that.

Tianna grew more determined. "You *will* show yourself. You *will* stand before me. I am Tianna, Priestess of Libran."

A strange sucking sound filled the air, then with a final pop, the being she had summoned forth did in fact stand before her, and he was not at all happy about it. "What is this? How dare you? How *could* you?" The self-proclaimed god looked down at her, the eyes on his equine head narrowing in anger and comprehension as he recognized the girl. "Yes. I know how you did it. So you have *finally* come into your power. None of us thought that you actually would, or even could, *human*. You've made enemies now of the gods. All but one. Do you really think he can protect you? Do you really think he *intends* to?"

Ignoring the question, Tianna gazed upon the splendor of the being she had summoned. There was a golden glow about him. He stood perhaps seven feet tall, with the body of a man, the head of a horse, and hands and feet that seemed at once both human and hoof-like. His entire body, aside from his hands and sandaled feet, was covered with short, brown fur. His armor was like none she had ever seen in her life. And of course he had wings; wings like Libran's. She steadied herself and remembered her purpose. "You are now under my power, *Guardian*. I will not release you until I have my questions answered both fully and honestly, and if you lie to me, I will know it. I need not fear the gods, for the gods must all fear *me*."

"Foolish human slime!" Centaurus moved then, lunging towards her, but an invisible force field sparked when his body hit the boundary set by the stones. He looked down with a snort and kicked at them, only to have his foot singed by another jolt from the invisible wall. "This cannot be."

"It is," Tianna said flatly. "You are my prisoner, and you shall remain in my power until I am satisfied that you have told me all that I wish to know."

Centaurus laughed, resigning himself. "I play the fool now for ever having doubted that this day would come. You are a monster now, albeit in human form. You will never lead a normal life, no matter what your desires may be." He studied her. "Yes, I have seen how your eyes linger on the form of Prince Joryn."

Tianna laughed. "He is pretty, I confess. But I am a priestess. I may idly enjoy the beauty of some mortal flower, but it is never to be, whether I am a monster now or not. Besides," she added with a knowing smile, "he has no taste for girls."

"From where I'm standing, I cannot say that I blame him," Centaurus grumbled.

"From where *I'm* standing, mighty Centaurus," Tianna continued, "I find myself disappointed in deities, judging from your example. For, if you have watched me closely enough to see my fleeting attractions, then you must have watched Joryn closely enough to know of his proclivities as well. You bait me. You only prove by this pathetic attempt how very much under my power you now are."

Centaurus raged. "I am under no mere *human's* power!" He caught his breath and realized this was, of course, precisely the case. "No *mere* human. You have *great* power, Priestess. Would you not like to know from whence these powers came?" He saw the uncertainty flash upon her face in the instant before she caught herself and recovered her composure. He grinned with the satisfaction of what he had discovered. "So, Libran didn't tell you. Well, how can I blame him, after all? A tiny human brain can only take in so much revelation in a day without collapsing. Besides, mortals only get to know what they *need* to know. Even rebellious Libran follows this one tenet. You are not worth wasting the truth on. Not to Libran anyway."

"Silence!" Tianna shouted, partly afraid of learning more than she should like to know, partly afraid of letting herself listen further and lose her resolve.

"What if I could tell you *why* you have the power that you do, young priestess? What if I could tell you *why* Libran hasn't told you himself? What if I could tell you everything that Libran is hiding from you? Would you release me then? Would you be satisfied? For I can deliver, just as I say." He watched her shrewdly, waiting.

She looked away, then returned her gaze to him. "No. Enough of this. I want to know what dealings you have had with the warrior Drae Shivvan. What is your investment in the invasion of Chiroptera?"

"I'd confess if I were you, horse face," suggested the iron bird in the rafters. "The priestess may yet have more power than she has revealed."

Centaurus looked up to where the voice had come from, with a sneer. "Iron Bill. Slumming it down here among the mortals now, are you?"

Tianna lost her patience. "Answer me *now!*" With a force of will, she filled the force field prison with psychic lightning that shocked and burned the Guardian held within.

"Mercy! Stop this! I'll tell you everything! I'll tell you *everything!*"

Tianna calmed, and so did the storm within Centaurus' prison. "Drae Shivvan," she prodded.

Grudgingly, head downcast, the Guardian confessed. "Five years ago, Shivvan's brother was killed in battle by a Chirop named Nightstorm. Ever since then, he has been petitioning me for vengeance. He even built me an altar. How could I refuse after five years of faithful prayer? So I appeared to him. I gave him my mark. I promised him revenge. I promised him the blood of Nightstorm."

"So you sent the Chirops to steal the crops of the Highlands?"

"Not exactly, Priestess. I did silently and invisibly *influence* their king however, and he offered up little resistance, succumbing to temptation almost instantly. But the decision was King Orlok's in the end, not mine. So you see? That is my involvement. I am simply honoring a humble servant who desires blood for his brother's death."

"No. There's more. You are one of the Twelve, and gods or no, we all know that the Twelve never assist a mortal without some motive of their own. So tell me. What did *you* get out of it?"

"Why, Priestess, you give me so little credit! Can a god not simply be magnanimous towards his worshippers?"

The lightning began to generate above him, flashing and crackling, reminding him of the pain she could give him.

"All right! All right! You're right! I demanded only one thing in return!"

Tianna folded her arms and waited, the lightning in the prison abating. "Well? What was this price you demanded of your loyal servant?"

He watched her closely, knowing now what she was capable of, finding himself resentful of the fear she had managed to instill in him. He knew his answer would upset her, but he also knew what would happen if he refused to comply. "It was nothing less than the head of Libran's champion. If I enabled Shivvan to kill Nightstorm, which I have certainly done, then he would repay me for my generosity by seeing to it that the brat prince of peace, Joryn of Nod, never returned from the battle!"

Tianna gasped. It was worse than she'd imagined. She had known that Shivvan had been concealing something, that he had made a bargain with Centaurus, but she only supposed he had meant to break his word to the prince, not murder him on the battlefield as payment to his dark god.

Centaurus laughed. "What's the matter, pretty? Did I say too much?"

"Be gone!" She waved her hand, and the Guardian vanished in an implosion of light, accompanied by the same strange sounds that had brought him forth. She kicked the rocks, breaking the circle.

Iron Bill flew down to her then. "You've made a powerful enemy just now."

"The enmity was already there," she said pointedly. "I simply uncovered it. At any rate, he has more reason to fear and puzzle over me now than I do him."

Overwhelmed by how extremely her life and world view had been altered in such a very small amount of time, Tianna struggled to form a plan. Only hours before, she had never seen a god. Now she had seen two of them, she knew that they were not, in fact, gods at all, but powerful beings called Guardians, and to top it all off, she had captured one, struck him with lightning, and banished him from her presence all with the previously unknown power of her will. It was unfathomable, but she had no time at the present to give it any more thought than that.

She looked to the communicator that she wore on her left wrist. Kabed had made it for her long ago and told her that if she ever needed anything, he would be there at the other end, waiting to serve her. He had become a friend since then, always looking out for her. She knew she could count on him to get the message to Joryn. She activated the device. "Kabed! Kabed! Are you there?"

No answer came.

"Maybe he's out of range. I don't know enough about how these things work." She sighed. "I have to get word to him somehow."

Iron Bill met her eyes, and as she smiled with remembrance, his mechanical eyes seemed to smile as well. "Did I mention, Priestess, that I can fly at near the speed of light?"

"Go, Bill! Tell Kabed! You have to get word to Joryn without alerting Drae, and I suspect Joryn and Drae are together at the head of the army. Kabed can get word to Joryn discreetly. He's very trustworthy and clever. You must get word to him at once."

"How shall I know him, Priestess?"

"He'll probably be riding a mechanical unicorn and almost certainly flirting with a beautiful woman, if there are any around him. I suspect he'll be near the others of Joryn's elite: a centaur, a Celestian, and a rather ill-tempered Lowland Elf."

Iron Bill nodded. "That sounds fairly distinguishable. I shall get word to him at once and do my best to protect the prince thereafter."

"Thank you, Iron Bill." She kissed him on top of his shiny head. "And be very careful yourself. We've only just met, and I look forward to enjoying your friendship."

"Indeed, Priestess. I shall return." With that, Iron Bill spread his wings heroically and flew straight out into the sunlight, gathering speed until he had vanished from sight, a loud thunder-clap sounding in his wake as he broke through the sound barrier and continued to gain momentum all the way to Chiroptera.

CHAPTER 8:
LIBRAN'S INFLUENCE

LIBRAN APPROACHED THE BREAKFAST CAMPFIRE BURNING in the Chiropteran wilderness, disguised in his customary hooded robe that hid his majestic wings and undeniable countenance. This was the last nudge he would be making on Joryn's behalf this day, and, as always, it was a necessary one. Necessary for the balance.

The young, dark-haired, tan-skinned human and the scaly, green-skinned reptisaur looked up from the meat they were cooking on sticks, noticing him. The cybernetic life form standing behind them didn't pay the stranger any mind, concerned only with the food on the sticks that its friends were preparing.

The young human offered a cautious greeting to the new arrival. "Hey there, buddy. Need anything?"

Libran spoke warmly, "Longshot, Trig, and Lowgun, I greet you as a friend."

At this, the young man put down his stick beside the fire, and his cybernetic horse ate the meat and the stick the moment the young man stood up.

The reptisaur kept cooking but watched Libran with his keen reptilian eyes.

"Now how is it you know who we are," the young man asked cautiously.

"I know of your recent flight from Mech Valley." Libran looked to the mechanical horse that now stared greedily at the reptisaur's meat, as if hoping it would drop without the lizard man's notice. "I know every detail in fact, Longshot."

The young man drew one of the two guns at his sides with lightning speed, smiled, and adjusted the large brim of his hat with the other hand. "You better be careful, pal. We aren't exactly in good standing with anyone who should be in the know about that. What do you want from us? Did the Mech Authority send you?"

Libran laughed. "No. I'm here on my own authority. I mean you no harm. I only wish to advise you. I know you're looking for a posse to go back into the valley and make a rescue. I know you've had no luck at all in this endeavor, and I know where you can find a group of heroes, like yourselves, who would be eager to take on your cause as friends."

Longshot looked to the reptisaur. "What do you think, Lowgun? Do we hear him out, or shoot him?"

The lizard man pulled his stick away from the fire, shot his long tongue out and pulled the cooked meat into his mouth, much to the disgruntlement of the stomping robotic creature beside him. "I say we hear him out," he said after swallowing. "Then we can shoot him."

Longshot looked doubtfully at the robed man. He scrunched up his nose, considering. "So what concern is it of yours, stranger? We don't even know you."

"I'm concerned for the heroes you will find just over those hills." He nodded to the west. "I have a very keen interest in the success of their leader, and I've been watching you. You three are just the allies he needs at his side right now. It would be of mutual benefit to both groups."

"All right, I may be a year shy of twenty," Longshot said, "but I've been around, buddy. I'm not taking any bait until I see there's no one dangling a hook." He aimed his gun at Libran. "Who are you, and why do you know so much about us?"

The lizard man, Lowgun, stood next, slowly reaching over his shoulder to pull the laser bow from his back.

Libran drew back his hood and removed his robe, unfurling his wings, revealing his powerful countenance to the three campers. "I am Libran, and over those hills is Prince Joryn, my champion. He has a group of elite warriors at his side in the battle that is about to unfold, but he will need you as well."

"Son of a ..." Longshot was nonplussed.

His robotic horse, Trig, reared up and whinnied at the sight.

"Calm down, Trig," the young man soothed. He holstered his gun and regarded Libran sternly. "I don't believe in the gods."

Libran laughed warmly. "And neither should you. Not the so called 'gods' of the Mountain of the Twelve anyway. There is an infinite being who created us all, but the gods of Nod are a lie. And the term 'god' really doesn't do justice to the Infinite. I am simply a friend who serves the balance of Nod, and I am offering you a gift in the friendship of these warriors over the hills. The choice is yours, Longshot. Make it well." With that, Libran rose into the sky and flew out of sight in the blink of an eye.

Longshot looked to his companions. "Well … that was different."

"That was a god," Lowgun said reverently, hooking the laser bow to the armor on his back.

"Said he wasn't," Longshot argued.

"It was Libran though."

"Yeah." Longshot went to Trig and patted him on the neck. "Everybody thinks he's a god, but he said he wasn't. Only a man of honor would do that. A man free from corruption. And I'm inclined to trust such a man."

Lowgun shrugged. "It makes sense. So are we packing up and heading out?"

"You know it, bro. Adventure calls!" Longshot pulled himself up and onto Trig's saddle. "Let's ride! Fire up the *Dragon Racer!*"

"Sounds like a plan." Lowgun got onto his own unique, wheeled vehicle and revved the engines.

Trig blasted a fire extinguishing foam from a compartment in his chest onto the campfire, reared up, and ran with amazing speed towards the distant western hills, followed by Lowgun in his souped-up *Dragon Racer.*

From high above, Libran watched with satisfaction, as the test of heroes started to unfold.

CHAPTER 9:
THE BATTLE OF CHIROPTERA

A S THEY RODE INTO THE LAND OF CHIROPTERA, A VOICE spoke into Drae Shivvan's ear, "Hear me, my servant!"

Fear and awe filled the warrior from the Highlands, as he whispered, "Yes, mighty Centaurus. I listen and obey."

"A troublesome mortal in the Kingdom of Nod has made it a priority to undo my purpose here. You must take care. Keep Libran's champion away from any messengers." The voice grumbled, "Especially strangely built birds. I shall motivate the hearts of Chiroptera's warriors and manipulate the battle as I can. If you get the brat prince alone, I shall see that he is killed. You need only stand aside and allow it to happen.

"At the same time, your enemy Nightstorm shall fly above your head, and you will go after him, removing you from the scene of your ally's death.

"Meanwhile, stay by the prince's side at all times. Work from the start to separate yourselves from the others. I will help you as chances arise. All will go according to my plan."

"Yes, Centaurus. A way to get Prince Joryn away from the others has already been placed in my lap." Drae chanced a glance in the prince's direction to be sure the young man had not heard. Joryn only seemed determined, as he rode beside his newly arrived siblings. Drae would have to separate the young royals, and soon.

He heard a commotion behind him, and he turned to see his warriors distracted by the approach of an eagle, which seemed to be targeting their group. They all laughed with nervous relief, when the bird landed right on the head of one of Joryn's men's steeds. " 'Especially strangely built birds,' " he repeated under his breath. He didn't know about "strangely built," but the bird's sudden arrival *did* seem strange.

A shadow fell over the army then, darkening the sky even more so than the ominous clouds that loomed at all times in the kingdom of Chiroptera. Drae looked up and saw that the bat people were making a defensive strike before they had even been attacked, swarming forth from the caverns of their mountain. He saw an opportunity to speed things along. "My prince! There will be no parley, and we cannot risk letting those Chirops get close enough to ask. If they do, blood *will* be shed. Our blood. Please, take me at my word, and let us ride together to show our warriors courage!"

Joryn looked to the sky and the countless advancing Chirops, and he knew that Drae was right. "I will not risk the lives of our people any more than I must. Your word is good enough for me."

Drae looked to Hero and Vail. "Will you give the order to charge ahead? The battle is now!"

Joryn nodded to his sister and brother, then turned his attention forward. "Let's ride, Illium! Stun cannons out!" Joryn drew the magnificent Sword of Libran then, and Illium and Shilo charged ahead with great speed, carrying the two brave war commanders into the rocky battlefield, Illium firing into the sky without prejudice, hitting several Chiropterans as they swooped down at the heroes, and opening the battle for all.

Behind them, the voices of Princess Hero and Prince Vail could be heard together, urging their warriors on into battle.

"Listen to me!" Iron Bill persisted.

Shaking his head in bewilderment, Kabed dismounted his Unitron and took the two light guns from the holsters at his sides, checking to make sure the weapons were set to stun. "Guns out, Marley."

The fully robotic unicorn complied, revealing Deluvian light cannons from compartments at its sides, just like Illium's.

Kabed removed his Aeropack from the Unitron's hind quarters then slapped the mechanical steed on the behind. "Now, go into battle. Stun as many of the Chirops as you can!"

"Command acknowledged," the Unitron said in an undeniably synthetic voice, just before bolting away and joining the fray.

Kabed strapped the Aeropack to his back and began to fasten the buckles on his chest and abdomen. He spoke to the persistent bird, "Now, you have very little time for me to listen, my friend. I'm just a bit preoccupied at the moment."

Bill looked to the Highland Elf woman standing several feet away and doing the same as Kabed with her own flight pack, patting her klomper and sending it into its shell. She winked in Kabed's direction and offered him a glowing smile. The bird looked back to the man. "With her, or with getting into that strange jacket of yours?"

"A little bit of both, if you must know. But here it is, and I'm talking to an *extinct* bird. A Deluvian war bird, if I'm correct? To what do I owe the honor? Oh, and, am I by any chance ... hallucinating?"

"No hallucination, Kabed of Deluvia. I am called Iron Bill, the last of my kind, sent from the priestess of Libran to deliver a most urgent message."

"Tianna? Is she all right?" Kabed's concern for the girl seemed to outweigh his other distractions altogether.

"She is better than you can imagine, sir, but her news regards Drae Shivvan. The priestess has discovered a plot to undo your prince. Drae made a deal with Centaurus, and his bargain requires him to see Joryn—"

Just then, three Chirop females landed and, without pause, slashed at the ground warriors who were still getting into their Aeropacks.

Unprepared, the warriors had put down their guns and could only dodge or raise the shields that were strapped to their arms as part of the Aeropack attire.

Kabed grabbed his guns and blasted the Chirop women without hesitation.

The three Chirop warriors collapsed instantly before him.

"Yeah. I was right," he said to himself, as he looked over the unconscious warriors, taking in their features. "I won't be making the moves on any of the bat ladies anytime *ever.*"

He turned to his fellow fliers. "Guns out, everyone. This battle's on. Engage Aeropacks." He hit a button on the contraption's shoulder, and its compact jet engine fired behind him, lifting him into the air.

The other seven warriors with Aeropacks, including Onri Sprigg, followed his lead.

Bill sighed. "Oh, how I've missed dealing with humans for the past three thousand years." He shook his head in exasperation. "Now I'm sitting on a rock and talking to myself. Sarcastically at that. Well," he said, stretching out his glistening wings, "clearly I need this." He took to the air in pursuit of his mission, catching up with Kabed in no time at all.

Kabed expertly maneuvered with his artificial wings, meeting warrior after warrior in battle. He quickly figured out that the best way to get around the enemies' shields was to fire both guns at them, pointed in two different areas, so they could only block one of the beams at a time, and he was pleased to note in person that his research into Chiropteran biology had been correct. The bat warriors had an involuntary defense mechanism that kept them alive, if they happened to fall asleep during long flights, that was triggered by the stun rays. Whenever one was shot, their wings spread out, gliding the unconscious creatures to the ground safely.

"You mad quack of a mechanic!"

Kabed dared half a glance beside him to see the diminutive Lowland Elf Onri Sprigg struggling with the Aeropack he'd been assigned. "Trouble, Onri?"

"This blasted, goat-drinking monstrosity strapped to my back was designed for someone *three times* my size!"

"Are my adjustments not doing the trick then?" Kabed fired off a shot, hitting yet another of the seemingly endless number of Chirops in the air with them.

"It's not the straps, man! It's the wings! They're too big!"

"You'll adjust, my friend. You're doing fine."

"Whatever, snot gobbler! If I die, I shall *kill* you!" The little elf flew off, firing his own light guns at the enemy.

Iron Bill approached Kabed then. "As I was saying …"

Kabed gasped in surprise. "Don't do that! I wasn't expecting a voice *right* by my ear up here." He raised his shield as a Chirop warrior came up beside him and struck down hard with his sword. Kabed was knocked downward by the blow, but managed to fire back at the enemy, hitting him square in the chest. "As you were saying?"

"Centaurus—," Bill began again.

"The *god* Centaurus?"

"Well, not to argue semantics, but I suppose so, yes. He has promised vengeance to Drae Shivvan, on a Chirop called Nightstorm, in return for the death of Prince Joryn on the battlefield."

"*What?*"

"I said, he has promised—"

"I know what you said. I was just taking it in. You're sure?"

"Positive."

"And you really were sent by the priestess?"

"I was. How can I prove it to you?"

Just then five Chirop warriors surrounded them. Kabed shot one down, but the others raised their shields and flew at him with their swords.

Iron Bill flew above them, dismissed as a mere bird. From behind, he circled them so quickly that they could not react, blasting them with powerful stun rays from his eyes.

Kabed regarded the bird with a nod. "That's proof enough for now. You are indeed an ally, Iron Bill. I will get to Joryn as soon as I can."

"The priestess thought you could get word to the prince discreetly. She was worried about Shivvan learning that his plot was discovered."

"Indeed," Kabed agreed. "Though, there may not be time for discretion at this point. I'm afraid the elf has attached himself to our prince for the duration of the operation. Thank you, my friend. I'm sure I will have many more questions for you after the battle. Assuming we both survive. These numbers are nearly insurmountable."

"Well, it *is* their territory."

"Agh!" came a cry from behind them. "Butt-belching gutter slugs! I am undone!" bellowed the Lowland Elf a short distance away, having just been struck from behind by the sword of a Chirop warrior.

Kabed turned to see Onri's Aeropack smoking as the little warrior spun around, descending rapidly. "Hold on, Onri! I'm coming!"

Another Chirop warrior cut Kabed off then, and the Deluvian was forced to stop and raise his shield.

"I've got him," Bill offered, swooping down after the falling elf.

"Good!" Kabed shouted. He got out from behind his shield and made to fire at the fiend, only to have the gun knocked out of his hand by the warrior's sword, which only just missed the Deluvian's fingers as he lost his grip on the weapon. Unable to position the second gun in his shield hand for a shot, Kabed was forced to punch the Chirop with his fist and hope for the best, which failed to manifest.

The warrior only grinned at Kabed, clearly unfazed by the punch and reacting to the blood now dripping down his face as though it were merely sweat. He swung his great sword at the Deluvian again and again, each time Kabed blocking with his more and more heavily dented shield.

At last, Kabed flipped backwards, avoiding the sword, and kicking the warrior in the face with all the might of his well-muscled legs. He then grabbed the Chirop's wrist behind the hand that held the sword and twisted sharply, before the winged enemy could recover. He grabbed the sword right out of the warrior's hand and knocked him on the head solidly with the hilt, then tucked the sword into his own belt. The Chirop warrior was dazed, flying lopsidedly, but still in the fight. Kabed took advantage of the winged warrior's momentary disorientation to switch his second gun over to his right hand. He aimed at the wounded bat man, readied to pull the trigger, then promptly hit him over the head with his shield instead, resulting in a loud, satisfying clang.

He watched as the warrior's wings spread out, gliding him safely down to the ground below.

The Highland Elf girl he had been flirting with flew up to him then, cocking an eyebrow with a questioning look.

Kabed shrugged. "That way just seemed like more fun. And as it turns out, it was."

The elf warrior laughed her agreement, and they flew off together in search of further combat.

Iron Bill, meanwhile, had grabbed Onri Sprigg by the belt straps of his flight pack and was busily tearing them away with beak and talons.

"What are you doing you deranged buzzard?" Onri shot the bird with his stun rays, not for the first time since he'd been rescued.

"Please stop shooting me, elf. You should already have noticed it has no effect. I'm made of Deluvian steel."

"As are my guts, you vile, flesh-eating chicken! You'll not have me for a meal! I am Onri Sprigg! Hero of the Lowland Elves!"

Iron Bill made one last slash at the belts with his talons, freeing the elf from the ruined Aeropack and letting the contraption fall to the ground, where it exploded on impact. The eagle then spun Onri around and gripped him by the shoulders. "Hold on to your guns then, hero. If you're as brave as they say, I shall carry you back into combat."

Onri laughed triumphantly. "Indeed I am! You've heard of me then?"

"Of course, Onri Sprigg," Bill confirmed. "I've read your trilogy."

"This is where we part ways," Joryn said to Illium, dismounting and getting into his Aeropack.

"Good luck to you, Joryn." Illium winked.

Joryn nodded, looking towards the mountain. "Yes. I'm sure gonna need it." He patted the unicorn on the neck. "Good luck to you too, old friend."

Illium smiled with his eyes and took his leave, falling in with Dorran Equus and Hero on her borrowed Unitron as they ran past.

Beside Joryn, Drae patted Shilo, and the long-necked, many-legged klomper drew into his shell to wait out the battle in safety.

"Are you ready, my friend?" Drae asked the prince.

"As I'll ever be," Joryn answered.

"Wait!" Vail rode up to them on his purloined Unitron and dismounted quickly. He went to Joryn and hugged him tightly around the neck.

Joryn laughed with delight and amusement. "What is it Vail? Are you so sure I'm not coming back?"

Vail pulled back and patted the slightly younger man on the cheek. "No. I'm just proud of my brother, and I want you to take all of my good faith with you into that mountain. I might not see you again until the conflict has ended ... and I wanted you to know. You're an inspiration, you know. To all of us."

Joryn laughed again and shook his head, not sure how to respond. "Vail ... go stun some bats, Brother. You can take even more good faith from me into battle." He hugged Vail again, then turned to Drae, who had been watching the scene with solemn reverence. He nodded at the Highland Elf, then hit the ignition control on his shoulder and sped into the air by way of his winged Aeropack.

Drae nodded to Joryn's brother. "Fight well, my prince." Then he did as Joryn had done, launching into the air himself and catching up quickly to Joryn as they made their way to the mountain, struggling to rise above the battle to the best of their ability.

Not far away, Nightstorm had been watching. He looked down to prince Vail, as the prince got back into the saddle of his Unitron and they both resumed firing at Nightstorm's warriors with great zeal.

Nightstorm turned to his second, Shadowrend. "I see an opportunity to demoralize Libran's champion. If we can drown the leader of Nod's army in despair, we can gain the greater advantage over his forces."

Shadowrend nodded his approval, eying Vail. "Agreed. Shall I kill him in front of Prince Joryn?"

Nightstorm put a hand out to stop his second from diving. "No. I'll take this one myself. I am thirsty, and royal blood is sweet. Whether Joryn sees the deed or only hears of it, he will be broken all the same." He smiled, zeroing in on the young prince and his Unitron.

"As for you, Shadowrend, start pulling warriors aside to work in teams. Have them lift boulders into the air and drop them on the forces of Nod. These light weapons they are using are a terror, but we *can* fight back. The boulders should block our warriors from the ground weapons, just as surely as they will snuff the weapons out. They only need to watch out for the humans and elves in the air, but there are so few of them that you can easily cover up the boulder crews from their notice."

He spoke to the warriors that flew at his back. "Cover me!" Nightstorm dived down in pursuit of Prince Vail, surrounded by his warriors.

"As you command, Nightstorm." Shadowrend said, as he watched the group swoop down. He then flew off on his own to start gathering warriors for the task he had been given.

On the ground, the majority of the warriors from Nod and the Highlands had yet to come physically near to any of their winged targets, and the battle was going well. Orders were passed down by Joryn and Drae as they made their way directly to the mountain in the air.

The centaur Dorran Equus was having the time of his life, firing into the air and bringing down bat warriors left and right. "Illium," he said, "this is great sport! Almost no challenge at all!"

Illium snorted, as he blasted a cluster of Chirops out of Joryn and Drae's aerial path. "Be careful not to grow too over-confident, my friend. Still, I must say it is a good stretch of the legs."

Dorran laughed, until a loud thud sounded behind him that he felt shake the ground. He turned around and saw a boulder that hadn't been there before. "Uh, Illium … I think you were right."

"What is it?"

"They've figured a way to compensate for not having any projectiles."

The Unitron Marley ran up to them then, warning in his blatantly synthetic voice, "Danger detected! Danger! The Chirops have—" He was cut off instantly as a boulder landed directly on top of him and smashed him into the ground.

"Gods! Marley!" Dorran turned and looked above, where he saw several groups of Chirops carrying boulders into position. "Illium! What would you suggest? If we shoot them down, they drop the boulders anyway!"

"Yes, so we dodge the falling rocks. It's our only option."

"Well then," a new voice broke in, "start dodging, buddy! Trig, switch!"

Illium and Dorran barely had time to take in the stranger riding a mechanical horse over the hills beside them, before he leapt off of the horse and landed on his feet, while the horse itself jumped into the air, reconfigured itself into an enormous gun, and landed clamped to the young man's back, with the giant gun barrel positioned over his shoulder and traveling the length of his arm. The man fired the massive gun into the air and started bringing down boulder-carrying Chirop clusters in all directions while shouting, "Yee-haw!" at the top of his lungs.

"What is *that?*" Princess Hero asked, riding up to Dorran's side and regarding the new addition to their company.

"I have no idea," the centaur mused, "but he's on our side, so who cares? Yee-haw!" he parroted loudly, raising a fist to the new arrival.

When the immediate threat of boulders in their vicinity had been stopped, the young man again shouted the words, "Trig, switch!"

The gun along his arm then flew back into the air and reconfigured itself into a horse, landing firmly on the ground and standing on its metal hooves.

The man mounted up quickly. He tipped his wide-brimmed hat to Dorran and Hero. "Name's Longshot. This here is my horse Trig."

"That's some horse." Hero nodded in the steed's direction.

Trig whinnied, sounding pleased.

Longshot laughed. "Well, he's not exactly from around here." He looked into the distance. "More boulder-throwers over that way. I guess we should help them out?" He winked at Hero. "You sure are lucky we showed up to save your skins."

Hero rolled her eyes. "Oh save it for the ding bats, buddy. Where's Illium?"

Dorran pointed. "He's there, where Marley fell."

The unicorn was trying to roll the stone with his hind legs, to no avail. "We need to uncover him," Illium said. "He could still be functional."

"He's just a robot, Illium," Hero said. "We shouldn't take the time—"

She was cut off by the stamping and snorting of Trig.

"Oh, no offense, Trig," she demurred.

"None taken," Longshot assured her with a laugh, patting the horse on the neck. "Besides, this won't take any time at all." He waved behind him to another strange machine, and it sped over in their direction. Longshot pointed at the boulder, and a blast fired from the front of the machine, which had been fashioned in the shape of a dragon's head, and the boulder was disintegrated.

The wheeled machine pulled up to a stop, and a reptilian humanoid stood up from it to get a closer look at his handiwork.

Longshot gestured with a nod of his head. "This is Lowgun and his *Dragon Racer*. He's my side-kick."

The lizard man scoffed. "Business partner."

"Side-kick," Longshot repeated.

"Side-kick my tail!"

"If you're finished," Ton La said, approaching the group urgently. "Drae wants us to head northwest to take out those boulder-droppers."

"Of course!" Dorran bellowed joyously. "We can't have the battle leaving us behind."

The warriors all rode off, and Illium nudged the broken body of Marley with his horn. "We'll return for you, my friend." He took his leave then and rejoined the battle with the others.

All that the broken form of Marley had to offer in reply, however, was, "Damage … Assessing … Damage … Assessing …" over and over again for the duration of the battle, mildly concerned that something was wrong, but otherwise blissfully unaware of the full extent of what had been done to him.

Far away from his friends, Vail had taken up with a group of elves and was desperately trying to fight off the sudden onslaught of Chirop warriors that had fallen on them from the sky. The menacing winged warriors had gotten in close to them by making a wall of shields and heading, it seemed, directly for Vail and his Unitron.

The Highland Elves had come onto the scene, blasting away at the edges of the wall of shields and taking a few low-flying Chirops down at a time.

"I don't understand it," shouted one of the elves, who had introduced himself to Vail as Listrel. "It's like they want something else. They aren't attacking like the others have."

"Well, whatever they have in mind, good Listrel, let's see they never attain their goal!" Vail fired at the wall of shields, just as it suddenly broke off in four directions, sweeping the elves away. Unsure which way to look, Vail failed to notice the one Chirop warrior who had kept moving towards him with lethal determination.

Nightstorm grabbed Prince Vail with sudden violence, yanking him out of the Unitron's saddle and lifting him into the air, while the elves were all too occupied with enemies of their own to do anything about it.

The Unitron reared up and fired at Nightstorm with all of its cannons, proclaiming, "Danger! Danger!" until it assessed that the Chirop had carried Prince Vail too high to survive a fall and promptly ceased trying to shoot them down.

"Unhand me, vile coward!" Vail demanded, as he struggled to move into a better defensive position. "Fight me like a warrior, on equal ground!"

"I already did that, little prince," said Nightstorm smoothly, "and I snatched you up victoriously. As for 'unhanding' you …" he grinned malevolently. "Just a little higher."

"Aha!" shouted Vail. "You intend to drop me to my death! I had heard of such tactics being used by your spineless warriors! If only I could draw my sword, I'd make quick work of you here and now! But, alas, I've given my word not to shed your blood!"

Nightstorm was bewildered by the outburst. It was as though the young human wasn't afraid at all; not of being dropped, not of the Chirop who held him, nor even death itself. Could this really be just bluster, so close to certain doom? Or was there something the human knew that Nightstorm did not?

Suddenly, Nightstorm cried out in pain, looking down to see the human's teeth sinking into his arm. "Little worm!" He threw the man aside in the air and looked at the wound.

As Vail flew aside and began to drop, he taunted the Chirop, "Yes! It was I who fed on *your* blood! Sweet irony! I'm not finished with you, bat!"

Nightstorm shook his head in puzzlement, then flew towards the falling prince, still determined to glut himself on noble blood before dropping him to his death.

As he approached, Vail grabbed on impossibly to a passing Chirop and put his light gun to the warrior's temple. "Fly, winged devil! Fly towards that one over there!"

The Chirop looked to Nightstorm and shrugged, uncertain what to do.

Nightstorm approached, and Vail would not be taken again. "So! You choose to defy me?" the prince asked his captive in a patronizing tone. "Then I shall have to dismiss you, fiend." He pulled the trigger, stunning the Chirop unconscious and holding on as he glided down, firing his light gun at Nightstorm, who repeatedly dodged and blocked the blasts with his shield.

Iron Bill flew up to the prince then, carrying a very excited Onri Sprigg, who shouted to the young human, "Prince Vail! What in the name of rancid nougat—!"

"It's glorious battle, Onri Sprigg! And I shall emerge *victorious!*" With that declaration, Prince Vail leapt from his gliding, unconscious Chirop and into Nightstorm's arms, where he proceeded to punch the Chirop general in the face repeatedly, as the startled bat warrior struggled to get his bearings.

"That one's … crazy," observed Iron Bill.

"Yep. It's like he's been eating candy out of the casket."

Bill considered that. "I won't ask."

"Probably better that way. There's a reason I was so glad to leave home."

Bill fired at Nightstorm with his stun rays, but the Chirop had regained his composure and blocked the blasts easily with his shield, even as the eagle moved around him to get a better shot.

"I can't get a clean shot," Bill said. "And it's only a matter of time before that boy gets himself dropped like a bad idea."

"Yes indeed." Onri agreed, shaking his head at the seemingly unconcerned Prince Vail, now wrestling with Nightstorm in mid air. "I suppose you're going to have to put me down and rescue him, then. My shoulders are getting sore anyway." He grinned, as Iron Bill turned and headed down. "Still, you've got to respect his courage!"

"There's a fine line, Sprigg, between courage and insanity."

"Yes," the elf agreed, "but either one will do in times such as these."

"You have a point."

As Iron Bill and Onri Sprigg departed, Vail got a hold on Nightstorm's throat and squeezed.

The Chirop pushed him back easily, but Vail had latched onto him with his legs wrapped tightly around the Chirop's waist. Winded, Nightstorm wiped the blood from his brow, ignoring the stinging of his arm where the young prince had bitten him. "You have broken your word, little man. You had said that an oath prevented you from shedding my blood. You have abandoned your honor."

"Nonsense, cur! Those words were just good flowery fun. I actually only gave my word not to *kill* you!"

"I have had *enough* of this!" Nightstorm grabbed Vail's shoulders with all of his strength and yanked him away from his body, throwing him aside once again.

Vail shouted out defiantly and fired his light gun at the Chirop, as Nightstorm dived down past him and snatched him back up from behind.

Noticing the mountain wall that had been growing ever nearer to them, Nightstorm made the decision to end this by slamming Prince Vail's body into the rocky wall as quickly, and as many times, as he could, before at long last glutting himself on the young royal's blood.

As Vail found himself being accelerated towards the mountain wall, however, he noticed something that the Chirop general had missed. Setting his light gun to full power, disregarding the order to keep it on stun throughout the battle, Vail took aim at the rocks, just above the nest he'd spotted, and fired. "Aha! And now it ends, vile Chirop!" Vail laughed, as he calmly reset his gun to stun, seemingly unconcerned with how quickly they were approaching the mountain.

Before Nightstorm had even finished taking in the prince's words, ten fully grown terrorbirds flew out from beneath the spot that Vail had hit with his light ray. The enraged terrorbirds flew towards the perceived threat of Nightstorm.

He let go of Vail, who grabbed the general's belt and held on, preparing to take a shot at the Chirop.

When the birds hit Nightstorm, however, Vail lost his grip on both the belt and his gun and fell, plummeting towards the ground with no escape in sight.

It was then that Iron Bill swooped in and grabbed the prince by the shoulders.

"Thank the gods!" Vail breathed out.

Iron Bill asked, "*Now* you show fear?"

"I tend to overcompensate when I'm terrified," Vail confessed. "I can't let the enemy smell my fear."

"You were terrified then? That whole time that you were leaping around off of unconscious Chirops?"

"Out. Of. My. Mind."

"Well … *that* part, at least, was apparent."

"Just get me to the ground, blessed bird. I want to kiss it, before I throw up."

Unaware of the rescue of Prince Vail, Nightstorm drew his sword and defended himself against the ravenous terrorbirds. He managed to fell three of them, before the deadly female sunk her talons into his side. "No! I will not be killed by *birds* in a battle where the enemy refuses to take our lives!" He struck her naturally armored legs, until he finally let him go.

But terrorbirds were notorious for never letting up once they'd identified their prey. She came back at him, fending off the other six males from her nest, as she tried to make a meal of the Chirop.

Nightstorm blocked her claws with his shield and at last threw his sword straight into her heart.

As the giant bird cried out her last, disbelieving squawk, Nightstorm flew towards her, retrieving his sword, and turning to face the remaining terrorbirds.

It was then that Shadowrend and several Chirop warriors noticed his peril and flew to his defense, taking out the mighty birds with their swords, while Nightstorm caught his breath.

When it was over, Shadowrend flew to Nightstorm's side. "Are you all right, Lord Nightstorm? Can you go on?"

Nightstorm was dizzy. He had lost a lot of blood in the battle with the birds, and he honestly did not know if he could answer his second's question without passing out from the effort. "Shadowrend, are our warriors faring well?" He noticed that the other Chirop was refusing to meet his gaze.

"We had the element of surprise, briefly," Shadowrend answered, "but they know to look for the boulders now. They are taking us out slowly but surely." He looked away. "I have failed you. I deserve to die."

"No!" Nightstorm put a hand on Shadowrend's shoulder, by all appearances to offer him comfort and assurance, but in reality only to steady himself. "Use the clouds, Shadowrend. They can't see through the clouds."

"Of course! It will be done, my lord." The Chirop second was suddenly rejuvenated.

Nightstorm remained visibly fatigued, as he gave Shadow-rend his orders. "Take as many boulders as you can, and drop them all at once. Crush our enemies. Flood the mountain with their blood." Nightstorm breathed in deeply, then exhaled, as if simply weary, when he was actually hiding great physical pain. "Now, Shadowrend, I am leaving you in command. I go to make a report to King Orlok." In truth, of course, he meant only to find a ledge on Mount Chirop and gather his strength. He had set the final play in motion, and there was little else for him to do now but sit back and watch, regardless of his physical state. There was no shame in it, but he still preferred not to let the others know how badly he had been injured.

"As you command, Nightstorm."

Shadowrend and the others flew off to obey, and Nightstorm made his way quietly to Mount Chirop, though the closer he got to his destination, the lower he flew.

Joryn and Drae were now closer to the mountain than any of their companions. They were only able to keep in contact via the communicator on Joryn's wrist.

The Highland Elves were still staunchly refusing to take orders from Joryn, so Drae had to give orders directly, whenever there was an elf present to hear his voice at Kabed's end.

Joryn contacted Kabed one more time. "Kabed, we're near enough to the mountain. I'm giving you command of Nod's army until I return. We'll be going into the mountain right away."

"Got it," came Kabed's reply. "And what about Drae?"

Joryn nodded to the elf. "You'll have to leave a commander in charge as well. They won't listen to Kabed."

Drae maneuvered to where he could speak into Joryn's wrist communicator.

Before he could say anything at all, Kabed's voice came back over the speaker, quietly, as if he was trying not to be overheard by anyone at his end, "Joryn, there's something you should know. Drae is planning to—"

The sound of the rest of Kabed's words were drowned out by the rending of metal, as a sword tore through Drae's Aeropack. Focused on their communications, neither Joryn nor Drae had seen the Chirop warrior coming up behind Drae, who promptly dropped from his height, his damaged Aeropack sputtering and sparking as he fell.

Joryn quickly blasted the jubilant Chirop with his stun gun and dived down after the Highland commander. He maneuvered himself in front of the elf and grabbed him under the shoulders. "I've got you, my friend. Hold on."

Joryn landed them both on the ground at the base of the cavernous Mount Chirop, speedily taking off his own Aeropack and setting it aside, propping it against a large stone, along with his shield. "Here," he said, moving to help unstrap the damaged Aeropack from Drae's back. "No need to lug around the extra weight now."

"Thank you," the elf said. "You saved my life." *Why does he have to be so good? Why couldn't his friend have finished warning him about me?* Realizing that Joryn's friends were onto him, Drae knew that he had to act fast. If Centaurus didn't make things happen the way that he'd promised, then Drae would have to kill the young prince himself. He looked at the youthful hero before him, as the young man set the elf's sparking flight pack on the ground. Drae wondered briefly if he really had it in him to let this heroic friend die, and he knew that he would simply *have* to, when the moment arrived. Lin *would* be avenged, or this whole operation would have been in vain. Nothing else mattered. Nothing at all.

"There," Joryn said. "You okay?"

Drae saw a massive Chirop slowly walking up behind Joryn, sword raised above his head. He watched, mesmerized. *All you have to do is let it happen.*

At that moment, Miiko Quickwing bolted out of the air, knocking Joryn out of the way. The winged Celestian reached for the sword at his side to block the coming blow but could not situate himself quickly enough.

The Chirop warrior's sword came down, slashing across Quickwing's unprotected chest, and the Celestian fell, just as Drae shot the Chirop with a stun ray, dropping him where he stood.

Drae stood stunned, not at all sure what had just happened.

It was at that very moment that he saw his hated enemy, Nightstorm, flying overhead, towards the mountain. *Of course! He's reporting to the king. He's in command here. Taking down Nightstorm will end the battle, and now is my opportunity. Now could be my only opportunity.*

"Quickwing!" Joryn ran to his fallen friend.

"My prince," the Celestian gasped out weakly. "Is it bad?"

Joryn studied the wound. "I'm afraid so, Quickwing. The sword struck deep. I'm going to get you home. Celestia's not far from here. Your people can heal you." He stared in horror at the blood flowing from the wound across Quickwing's chest. "What happened to your armor?"

Quickwing struggled to remain conscious, as he answered, "A Chirop came at me from behind and unfastened it. We struggled, and I won, but I didn't have time to retrieve it from the ground before I saw you were in trouble."

"Thank you, Quickwing," Joryn offered solemnly. "Now it's my turn to save you." He looked to the elf. "Drae, I'm going to take the Aeropack and get Quickwing out of here. You'll have to take command of the operation. My people will listen to you."

"No," Drae said. "I'll take the Aeropack."

"But the elves won't listen to me or to Kabed. They'll only take orders from another elf. You have to be the one to stay."

"I intend to, Joryn," Drae said breathily, his voice full of guilt. He nodded to a ledge high above, where his target had perched, probably at a communication portal. He put a hand to the hilt of his brother's sword. "I'm going after Nightstorm."

Joryn was shocked, pleading through silent tears, "But Quickwing will *die* if we don't get him help right now!"

Just then, Onri Sprigg climbed over the rocks to greet them. "My prince! I just got dropped off and thought I would come and assist you at the mountain." He rubbed his shoulders, sore from the lengthy ride in Iron Bill's talons, and noticed that he was being completely ignored, that tears streamed down Joryn's face, that Quickwing was down, bleeding profusely from his chest.

"I'm taking him, Drae," Joryn said firmly. "I'm sorry. Your vengeance will have to wait."

"What's happening here," Onri asked.

Joryn stood and went for the Aeropack.

Drae drew his brother's sword and went to intercept him.

Joryn drew his sword as well, and Drae marveled at its beauty; truly the gift of a god.

"You know I won't kill you, Drae, but I will defend myself."

Drae had gone mad with desperation. This was his chance. His wild-eyed countenance was nothing like that of the noble elf warrior who had gone with Joryn this far into the battle. He was another man entirely now. "I *will* kill you, my prince. I *will* kill you. I must avenge my brother's death! That's what this was all about!"

Joryn noticed the glowing mark on Drae's arm then, recognized the Mark of Centaurus from his lessons with Parakletos, and suddenly everything clicked. "You ... You set this up. You made a deal with a god!"

His face twisted in agony, Drae confirmed it, "I had to! He killed my *brother*, Joryn! You have brothers and sisters to spare, but Lin ... Lin was my only one. He was my best friend, and that *monster* took him from me!"

Stunned by the revelation, Joryn continued, "Drae, you ruined your own people's crops. You *arranged* the whole incident to *start a war*, just to have your revenge! Quickwing could *die*, and who will avenge *him*? Who will avenge *Nightstorm* once you've murdered him? And then who will avenge *you* after that? Where will this end, Drae? I tell you vengeance *never* ends!" He pleaded, one last time, "Put down the sword, Drae, my friend. Put down the sword, and end this cycle of bloodshed here and now."

Tears streamed down Drae's face, as conflicting emotions battled within his heart, tearing at his mind. "I'm sorry, my prince." He struck without any more warning, and Joryn blocked the blow with the Sword of Libran, looking for a way to end the battle without killing the elf commander.

Onri went to Quickwing then and, kneeling down, took the Celestian's big hand in both of his little ones. "Stay with us, Quickwing." He looked to the duel of the war commanders. He knew that if he made his way around them to get a shot at Drae Shivvan, it might prove a fatal distraction for Joryn. He had to be patient. He held Quickwing's hand, and he waited for an opening.

As their blades crossed again and again, Joryn continued to plead with his unexpected enemy, "Drae, you *have* to let go of your wrath! You have to think of your people. You're their *champion*! It's your duty to put their needs first!"

"Perhaps that is the way of Libran, my prince." Drae crossed his sword with Joryn's one last time, pushing forward with his upper body and forcing Joryn to fall backwards over a pile of rocks. "I'm sorry." He pointed his brother's sword at Joryn's chest, shaking his head with remorse. "But Libran is not my god."

He dropped the sword then, drew his light gun, and turned on Onri Sprigg, pulling the trigger.

Onri fell, dropping his own light gun.

"I saw you waiting for your moment, little fool from the Candy Village." Drae holstered the gun, picked up his brother's sword.

Joryn was getting to his feet. He had dropped his own sword when he had fallen.

Drae took advantage of the moment, grabbed the prince, and spun him around, pressing him against the side of the mountain, his blade to the young man's throat.

"Drae Shivvan," Joryn forced out the words, "do not betray *yourself.*"

"Prince Joryn of Nod," Drae said, his face contorting once again in tearful turmoil, "you saved my life." He struck Joryn quickly across the head with the hilt of his sword and let go of him, watching the young hero drop to the ground in a heap.

Drae went for the Aeropack and strapped it on. He looked up to where Nightstorm was still perched on the ledge, watching the great battle in the distance. He ignited the Aeropack's engine and flew up to meet him.

"Joryn," the voice of Kabed rang out desperately from the communicator. "Where is Drae? His people have stopped moving. They haven't heard from him. They aren't doing anything but holding their ground. I need Drae to order them back into action! Joryn!"

Drae Shivvan flew towards his brother's murderer, transformed into an avenging angel. It was done. Centaurus had kept his word. "Nightstorm!" He landed on the ledge that jutted out from the side of the mountain, just above the lowest-hanging clouds. He took in the sight of his enemy. There was no communication portal. There was only Nightstorm, inexplicably removed from the battle.

The Chirop warrior turned his head with narrowed eyes. "I knew you would come for me, Shivvan. I should think you'd have learned, from your brother's mistakes, that I am not to be trifled with." He turned towards his enemy, holding a blood-soaked hand to his left side.

"You're wounded," Drae noticed.

"Yes. A flock of terrorbirds came out of a mountainside, determined to make a meal of me. Such irony, in a battle where the enemy refuses to fatally harm us, to be wounded by nature itself."

No coincidence, thought Drae. *Thank you, Centaurus. Victory is assured.* He gripped the hilt of his brother's sword. *Now to add one final chapter to the Saga of Lin Shivvan.*

Nightstorm drew his own wicked blade then. "I am as dangerous now as a wounded animal, elf! Let us do battle and see who is the more terrible. It matters not to me. Your people are going to die whether I live or not. Just look below and see for yourself."

Drae spared a glance, and then another. It was no trick. His people were holding their ground, but Chirops were coming at them from all directions in the air with their boulders, ready to crush the elves into oblivion, from above the clouds, where the forces on the ground would never see them coming.

"It doesn't matter," Drae said, more to himself than to Nightstorm. "All that matters is sending you to Hell." He drew Lin's sword.

"Then do! And I shall take you with me!" Nightstorm lunged at the elf with his sword, and Drae blocked, jumping back and pushing forward again with his own angry strikes, which the bat warrior deftly parried. Even wounded, the Chirop was formidable. It would take time to wear him down enough to strike the killing blow.

Time in which Drae's people would be massacred.

Drae stepped back, lowered his sword.

Instead of pressing his advantage, Nightstorm took the opportunity to catch his breath. "Second thoughts, my avenging elf?"

Drae's face twisted in anger, and he lunged at the bat warrior again, who proved no less efficient at defending himself than before. Drae knew all he had to do was wait Nightstorm out. The Chirop had lost a lot of blood. He was tiring. If Drae pressed on, vengeance *would* be his.

And his people would die. And who would avenge them? Who would avenge them against the one who had ignited this conflict in the first place? Who would avenge them against … him?

Drae backed away again, and Nightstorm caught his breath again and laughed mockingly. "You haven't got it in you, have you, little warrior?"

"No," Drae said, thinking of all he'd done. "I haven't got it in me to let my people die in order to satisfy my own lust for your death. I haven't got it in me to kill a warrior dishonorably, or to let heroes die. I haven't got it in me to waste one more minute here with you. But we will meet again, Nightstorm. Flee from this battle now, and know that we will meet again when duty is not so pressing."

Drae launched himself from the ledge and flew with the Aeropack towards the boulder-bearing Chirops, shooting two groups down from above before they were over their target and causing the people on the ground to notice the rest still approaching through the clouds.

Quickly Drae flew to Kabed and spoke to the Highland Elf at his side. "Sheidra, take command of the Highland forces *now*. Tell the ones with Aeropacks to fly into the clouds! They're coming from the clouds!"

Sheidra gave the command immediately, and the ground forces began firing into the clouds, just as the Chirops were starting to emerge.

Drae turned to Kabed then, having placed a hand on his shoulder to prevent the Deluvian from going bravely into the cloud battle himself. "I have to get back to the mountain. Joryn is down, and I need to rouse him. We *must* see the plan through."

Kabed nodded seriously and called out, "Iron Bill!"

The bird flew down and perched on his arm, "Yes, Kabed?"

"Joryn is down. Is it true what I've read, that war birds can heal with the same technology they use to destroy?"

"Oh, absolutely. Where is he?"

"At the base of Mount Chirop. Follow Drae." He nodded to the elf in question. "And recruit whoever that is down there who keeps shooting down great bundles of Chirops all at once. He could be the very thing we need to get Joryn into the king's chambers without being taken captive."

"If he hasn't been already," Drae noted with dread and self loathing. He bolted away towards the mountain.

Iron Bill followed, swooping down quickly to recruit the man with the giant gun. "You there!"

"You there yourself," said Longshot.

"You are needed at the mountain. Prince Joryn requires an escort with your talents to take the king's stronghold. I'll carry you."

"No need," the young man protested. "Trig, switch!"

Iron Bill backed up, as the enormous gun flew off of the man's body and reconfigured itself into a horse.

"Can he keep up?" asked the war bird.

"He can keep up. I'm Longshot, by the way, and this is Trig."

"Lovely. I'm Iron Bill. Follow me now. There is no time for pleasantries."

The bird took off, and Longshot laughed. "Pleased to meet you, Iron Bill. Let's go, Trig! Follow that bird!" The horse reared up and charged at a pace not even Illium could have matched.

At the mountainside, Drae found Joryn, Onri, and Quickwing where he had left them and chose not to take the time it would have required to breathe out a sigh of relief that they had not been captured. He landed and removed the flight pack, just as Iron Bill landed behind him.

The metallic eagle looked at Joryn and bathed him with a soothing blue light from his eyes. Joryn began to stir, and then Bill turned his attention to Onri.

Drae shook the prince, rushing his recovery. "My prince, I'm sorry. I was almost too late realizing what a fool I've been."

"Nightstorm?" Joryn asked groggily.

"Will live to fight another day," the elf answered somberly.

"Quickwing!" Joryn bolted up and went to the fallen Celestian's side, just as Onri got to his feet, rubbing his head.

"I'm sorry," Iron Bill said with a shake of his head. "I can't heal him. The wound's too deep. My healing ray only works on

minor injuries and reversing the effects of Deluvian light weaponry. There's still time though, if he can be moved."

"Here's the Aeropack," Drae offered. "Onri, can you——?"

"I will hear nothing from you, you villain!" He went to the
flight pack. "I will take the Aeropack, if someone can help me to
carry him."

"Of course," offered Iron Bill.

The little elf looked up to Joryn, anticipating his protest. "I
know you would do it yourself, but you are our best chance at
ending this conflict. You must get to the Chirop king, as
planned."

"Thank you, Onri," Joryn said with a smile. He helped to
fasten Onri into the flight pack, trying to make adjustments for
the diminutive warrior's size as well as he could. "Fly carefully."
He turned to the bird then. "And you ..."

"Iron Bill, sir. A friend of the priestess and of Libran himself."

"Man, that Libran sure knows how to put together a posse,"
Longshot said, as he and Trig arrived on the scene.

"He certainly does," Joryn smiled, then remembered. "The
sword!" He went to where he had dropped it and found it waiting
for him there to be retrieved.

"I didn't do it, Onri," Drae offered weakly.

"I know that," said the Lowland Elf. "But you're still a snot-
gobbler, and we'll settle the matter another time. For now, I must
put all of my fury into taking Quickwing to his people."

He looked to Iron Bill. "Do you know the way to Celestia,
birdie?"

"I know the way to everywhere," Bill assured him. Then, "Never call me that again."

"Fair enough. Let's go then."

With that, Onri grabbed Quickwing underneath the shoulders, and Iron Bill took hold of the Celestian's feet, and they carried the fallen warrior up into the air and onward towards Celestia.

Joryn sheathed his sword and glared at Drae, who looked away in shame. The prince then collected his shield from where he had left it against the stone and addressed the other new arrivals. "And you are?"

The man dismounted from his steed and tipped his hat with a wink. "I'm Longshot. This is Trig. Iron Bill thought we could be of service getting you to the king of the mountain."

"How's that?" Joryn asked.

Two Chirop guards, armed with spears, appeared at the mouth of the nearest cavern.

"Trig, switch!" The horse made his transition into a giant gun, and Longshot used it to stun both Chirops at once. "That's how."

Joryn laughed in spite of his anger at Drae.

"Joryn," Drae said meekly. "You still have my sword. My brother's sword."

Joryn said nothing in response, as he walked past the elf and into the mouth of the cavern, past the fallen guards. "Now we take the king."

"Yee-haw," Longshot shouted, following Joryn enthusiastically.

114

Not sure whether he had been invited or dismissed by the prince's silence, Drae Shivvan followed as well, no longer feeling like any kind of commander, no longer feeling worthy to be called a hero. Though his people may not yet have known it, he was no longer the champion of the Highland Elves, and he knew it terribly even if no one else ever learned the truth, as he had no doubt that they would.

Kabed and Sheidra oversaw the last sputters of fight in the Chirop ranks being put down, and Kabed tried once again to contact Joryn on the communicator. "Joryn, are you there?"

"Here, Kabed."

"Thank the stars! You're all right!" At this point, Hero, Vail, Illium, and Dorran drew close to listen to the conversation.

"Yes. Long story. We're moving on the mountain now."

Kabed heard the sounds of the strange warrior's giant gun firing and laughed. "I'd love to see the faces of those guards right now. I bet you're just walking right through them."

"Walking right through. I like this Longshot and his Trig. They can stay."

Kabed laughed again. "They brought another one who's not so bad either."

"I look forward to meeting him," Joryn said. "How go things at your end?"

Another blast sounded from Trig.

"We've actually pretty much mopped up," Kabed answered. "There wasn't much left to do after we took out that cloud ambush. The entire Chirop army, as far as we're aware of them, will be unconscious for hours. We're walking around the sleeping bodies everywhere. Surprisingly no casualties on our side. Except for my Unitron, but he can be repaired."

"Quickwing went down too," Joryn told him, "but Onri and Iron Bill are taking him to Celestia."

"Is it bad?"

Another blast from Trig echoed over the speakers.

Joryn was unfazed, proving that the conquest of the mountain was going their way. "It's bad, but Iron Bill seemed to think there was still time to save him if they got him off the battlefield."

"About Iron Bill," Kabed said. "I'm not sure we can trust him."

"What makes you say that," Joryn asked with concern. He had just trusted Bill with quite a precious cargo after all.

"The thing is," Kabed continued, "we would have been sunk out here if not for Drae Shivvan swooping in when he did, alerting us to a lethal ambush, and getting Bill and that kid with the enormous gun to go and help you at the mountain. So, Iron Bill may have given me some bad information that I almost passed along to you."

"He didn't," Joryn assured him flatly. "Bill knew what was up, and I discovered the truth for myself before you could warn me."

"Then what—?"

"As I said, long story, and we're at the king's chambers, so I'll have to fill you in later. Joryn out."

Excitedly, Vail drew his sword, as he'd been waiting to do throughout the entire battle. "It's over now," he beamed. "Time to draw our swords and wave them around as though we had used them! For dramatic effect!"

Kabed offered a sly grin to the elf woman with whom he'd been flirting throughout the entire battle. "Well, Sheidra, Joryn's about to do his talking thing, so how 'bout we let King Orlok hear our cheers of victory?"

The elf grinned brightly, and the two of them led their people in the loudest, wildest victory cheer they could muster, after which Sheidra kissed Kabed firmly on the lips; a move to which Kabed happily surrendered.

CHAPTER 10:
THE KING'S HONOR

KING ORLOK SAT DEFIANTLY IN HIS THRONE, LISTENING to the sounds of the approaching storm outside. When the door was finally blasted down, his two remaining guards ran to face the intruders and were quickly stunned by an enormous light ray. "I will *never* surrender!" he said to the clearing dust of what had once been a solid iron door.

Drae and Longshot stepped in then, aiming their weapons at the king.

Joryn stepped in afterwards, drawing the sword of Libran for dramatic effect and thinking of his brother Vail with a not entirely suppressed smile. "King Orlok of Chiroptera, your forces have fallen. We will now discuss the terms of our victory."

"There is no victory! You will have to kill me!" The king stood.

Joryn spoke with a magnificent strength that stopped the Chirop in his tracks and surprised himself as well, "Your fate will be the same as that of your warriors. I give you my word as a prince of Nod. But first, you *will* listen."

The king changed posture, willing to hear what the prince had to say, but added, "My people would rather die than be conquered and forced into the Empire of Nod. We will not become subjects of your father."

"We do not mean to conquer you, King Orlok. In truth, I offer you the hand of friendship, from the emperor of Nod."

"Then … you expect me to believe that you have taken all of my forces and my stronghold, and you *aren't* going to subjugate me? You *aren't* going to exact vengeance for what we did to the Highlands?"

"We've had enough vengeance for one day, Orlok," Drae put in.

Joryn silenced him with a look. "As I said, we offer you, a proud race who cannot surrender without losing your honor, a friendship between the kingdom of Chiroptera and all the kingdoms of Imperial Nod, in exchange for certain gifts to the emperor."

"What gifts?" The king asked cynically.

"We want the crops of the Highlands returned to them in full, plus ten percent of your own food stores, which are known to be in great surplus. We also ask, in the name of our new friendship, that you offer to aid us whenever any of our king-doms faces war from an outside force, and that you live in harmony with all of the kingdoms of Nod."

"And what *gifts* will the emperor offer to me?"

Joryn spoke pointedly, "Our friendship."

King Orlok understood what the cunning little prince was actually saying. The offer of friendship was, in fact, an offer not to annihilate them while they were under his power. The "gifts" to Emperor Sapros were actually cleverly rephrased terms of surrender, so that the king would never have to utter the word "surrender" to his people. He could walk away from this battle having negotiated terms of "friendship" and gained his kingdom an autonomous alliance with the Empire of Nod, which no doubt also included their alliance with the dragons of Din. The young prince was offering to let *everybody* win. It was unprecedented. There was to be no great public humbling of Chiroptera.

The king rubbed his chin thoughtfully. He reminded himself, staring at the Sword of Libran, that he was dealing with the alleged emissary of a god; the very same emissary who had brokered peace between Nod and the dragons. Perhaps it had even *actually* happened as the stories claimed. He had everything to gain by taking the offer, and he wouldn't even look weak in doing so. "I have your word, young prince, that the kingdom of Chiroptera will not be laid low, should I accept this offer of friendship and offer these gifts from our food stores to the emperor?"

"You have my word, King Orlok."

The king extended his hand. "Then you have our friendship, Champion of Libran."

Joryn sheathed his sword, stepped forward, and took the king's hand.

Drae and Longshot cautiously lowered their weapons.

The two leaders laughed; both in secret relief.

"I will have the harvest sent as soon as is possible," Orlok assured the prince.

"We will stand by, of course, to assist you in loading the klompers, until you are ready," was Joryn's shrewd reply.

The king gave pause, then laughed, as though this were a welcome offer. "Ah! Good, good! Then I am sure we will have your klompers loaded and on their way before the sun sets this day! I am eager for the emperor's friendship. In fact, in addition to these gifts he has requested, in my infinite generosity, I shall also offer a gesture: the banishment of the warrior Nightstorm from our kingdom, as he was the very fiend responsible for the unauthorized attack on the crops of the Highlands and the hostile welcome of your people when you came to extend the hand of friendship. Nightstorm will no more be welcome in the comforting darkness of our mountain!"

"That really isn't necessary—"

"But it is! It is!" The king slapped Joryn on the back in an all too enthusiastic gesture of camaraderie.

Joryn reminded himself that he couldn't save the entire world with a single victory. He thought about what he had learned of politics from his brother Kail. He was about to get everything he wanted from the outcome of this battle, with the only blemish being that a warrior he knew to be a pawn in the king's own schemes would be taking the full blame for the king's misdeeds. He couldn't risk undoing the return of the crops and the new alliance with the Chirops by arguing for Nightstorm's forgiveness. It was one of those times when he understood the burdens of a king, as Illium had taught him to see it. He had to put the multitudes before the individual. He had to choose his battles and fight them one at a time. "King Orlok, my friend, I thank you for your gracious offer on behalf of my father, the emperor of Nod."

Drae Shivvan watched this exchange with awe. The little prince had known what he was doing all along. He had spared every life in Chiroptera and secured an alliance that would come packaged with the silent gratitude of every warrior's would-be widow or widower, every warrior's child, every warrior's mother and father, as well as the grudging respect and gratitude of the Chirop warriors themselves. And Nightstorm had gotten his, without the sword of Lin Shivvan having gone through him. Nightstorm had been banished. It was done.

Drae put a hand to the Mark of Centaurus on his arm, as it was beginning to burn, but he decided not to let it show. The god was angry with him. There could be no doubt. Joryn still lived, and all of Nod was better for it. Drae would never doubt the young prince again.

CHAPTER 11:
WE NEVER GO HOME AGAIN

THE KLOMPERS OF THE ARMY OF THE HIGHLANDS WERE loaded with the requested "gifts of friendship" and carried both food and warriors home. The warriors of Nod stayed the night in the Highlands to celebrate their victory in the court of an astonished and jubilant King Rune.

Though Drae Shivvan spent the evening and most of the following morning in dread, Joryn never said a word about what had happened between them to anyone aside from Kabed, and Kabed was just as tightlipped about it as Joryn, following his prince's lead.

Drae tried to quiet his mind by focusing on the good fortune that had led to his father's swift recovery, but it did him little good. Others had not been so fortunate during the Chirop raid. His arm burned worse by the hour, and his conscience was destroying him even faster.

The warriors from Nod returned to their own kingdom late the next evening, having set out right after breakfast, and fed their exhaustion with much needed rest.

Two days after the Battle of Chiroptera, Iron Bill returned to Palace Nod with Onri Sprigg, reporting that Quickwing was recovering well, but was not yet well enough to leave the care of his physicians in Celestia.

As Prince Joryn awaited with dread an audience with his father, he and Onri struck up yet another game of Imperial Strata-Gem, and, to Joryn's surprise, the little warrior had yet to lose his cool. The two sat in serious contemplation of the game board, silently plotting against one another.

"They do this a lot you say?" Longshot asked.

Dorran yawned. "Yep. Ends the same way every time."

"You beat me!" Joryn shouted in surprised delight.

Dorran did a double take. "Wait! *What?*"

"That's right, royal sapling! Onri Sprigg is victorious at last!" The Lowland Elf jumped up onto the table and started wagging his rump in the prince's direction. "Smell my patootie!"

Joryn only laughed. "How did you do it, Onri?"

"It's like you said. I stopped focusing on attacking you and started focusing on my game strategy."

Joryn shook his head and smiled thoughtfully. "Somehow, I don't think I'm the one you really learned that lesson from, Onri."

Illium laughed at the scene. "Now if only you can teach him to *win* gracefully, we'll have ourselves quite a well tempered little elf."

"I have more patootie to be smelled, glue for bones!" Onri said. "Whiff the patootie! Do it now! I am victorious!"

The gathered friends all laughed, until they were interrupted by an unexpected guest.

The Highland Elf bowed lowly on the ground. "Prince Joryn, if you will hear me, I have much to say."

Joryn stood, surprised. "Drae Shivvan." A thousand emotions ran through his spirit, before he settled on what he had long since decided was the path to take with this man. "Stand up." He smiled. "I am not my father."

Drae did as requested and drew the sword of Lin Shivvan from the scabbard at his side.

The warriors gathered there all moved to grab their weapons, but Joryn stopped them with a wave of his hand.

Drae spoke then, "I may be accused of treason, but I say if you *were* the emperor, Imperial Nod would be better for it. You have shown me mercy that I did not deserve. You have shown me a way of facing my enemies that I never dreamt was possible. Your grace and forgiveness, knowing my deepest failings, is more than I can ever hope to feel worthy of, and I have found that I would serve the Highlands best by serving you." He held the blade out to Joryn across both hands. "I give you my sword,

Prince Joryn of Nod. And if you see fit to let me carry it at your side, may it never draw blood again."

Everyone stared at Joryn, none, aside from Kabed and Onri, aware of what had transpired between him and the Highland Elf on the battlefield.

Joryn smiled, glad he'd chosen forgiveness as the response to Drae's betrayal. He reached out and took the sword. "Drae Shivvan, you have proved yourself a noble warrior indeed, able to learn from his mistakes, and brave in the face of impossible odds. You saved Quickwing's life by making the choice you did. You turned the battle around and put your people ahead of your personal vendettas." He did not need to add that Drae had caused the near tragedy in the first place, because he knew by the elf's sickly presence that he was well aware of his own fault in the matter and of having almost caused Quickwing's death himself before his change of heart. But his heart *had* changed, and that was all that mattered to Joryn.

The prince met Kabed's eyes, and the other man nodded back at him. Joryn handed the sword back to Drae. "Take your sword, Drae Shivvan. I would gladly have you carry it at my side." He laughed. "And, true to your wish, may it never draw blood again." He patted the startled elf on the back. "Welcome to our merry band."

The group of heroes gathered around and welcomed him. Drae found himself grinning ear to ear in relief, having been certain that the prince would at last cast him in irons and lock him away in a prison until his death.

Longshot stood against a wall with Dorran and muttered, "Hell, that was regal. All I got for my trouble when we got here was, 'Hey, you hungry? Want some pancakes?' "

Dorran considered that seriously. "Oh, I would *love* some pancakes."

"Yeah," realized Longshot. "Me too. Skip regal welcomes, buddy. Let's go eat."

Dorran put an arm around Longshot's shoulders in friendship. "Kid, I think we're gonna get along great!"

One of the palace squires interrupted them then. "The king will see you now, my prince."

Everyone went quiet, and Joryn stood. He looked to Longshot, Trig, and Lowgun. "I can't bring up your matter in this meeting. He's going to be in no mood. But I will help you, Longshot. We'll discuss the matter further when I get back."

"Thanks, Joryn," Longshot said with a tip of his wide-brimmed hat. "I gotcha."

In the throne room of Palace Nod, Joryn took his place, standing directly before his father. He noticed his brother Kail was standing beside the throne, no doubt fully prepared to defend him. "Father," Joryn greeted the king with a half-bow. "You wished to see me?"

"Yes," his father said gruffly. "I want to know *why Chiroptera is not a part of our empire!*"

Joryn stood his ground, stalwartly. "Father, I will tell you."

"Well?" the king raged. "Go on! Astonish me with your pitiable excuses, whelp!"

Kail studied the countenance of his younger brother. He had apparently aged years in the past few days. He seemed to have no fear of their father, and it worried him.

Joryn answered his father's angry demands calmly, "I led your army into Chiroptera and took the kingdom without a single life lost on either side. I walked into the throne room of King Orlok with three men and took the royal caverns. I used my position as the would-be conqueror of Chiroptera to negotiate an alliance that would not come with the secret resentment of the Chirops.

"If I had subjugated them, if I had killed their warriors, if I had laid their king low, we may have added them to our empire, it is true; but by leaving them intact and autonomous, I have secured a powerful ally for our empire that bears us no ill will.

"In addition to this, I accomplished the objective you sent me out with. I reclaimed the crops of the Highlands, *plus* ten percent of the Chirops' own harvest, and allowed them to view it politically as a gift freely given in honor of our new alliance. Yes, I could have taken *all* of this by force and made Chiroptera bow to the Imperial Crown, but as subjects of Imperial Nod, they would have always been secretly plotting against the throne, would they not?

"I may be the youngest and least valued son of the emperor, but I have been at court my whole life and know the workings of kings who ever seek to outmaneuver and overpower one another, and I know that your anger stems not from the fact that Chiroptera was not subjugated, though I was not expressly ordered to do so, but from the fact that your most hated son has once again returned home *alive* from a mission it was hoped I would fail."

The king's face went beet red with rage, and Prince Kail stood beside him in openmouthed astonishment.

"I make this promise to you, Father," Joryn continued. "Send me on as many suicide missions as you like. Put my morals and my courage to the test. Put the lives of others on the line to *try* and erase the threat of my existence ... and I will return victorious *every single* time.

"I am the champion of Libran. It is true. Libran sent me further aid, in fact, in this very battle. But I am not a weaker man for my devotion to peace, and I am not a lesser man for accomplishing the same ends, with even better long-term results, as you would have had me do with violence and dominance. I am a man of peace, and oh yes, I am, at that, a *man*." Prince Joryn bowed to his father then and promptly left the room without having been dismissed.

Shortly thereafter, Prince Kail found his brother in the stables, brushing Illium's back, and just like that, he saw him not as the mighty general who had faced down their father, but as his vulnerable little brother again, in need of comfort and security. "Father loses his temper," Kail began, "and people die, or at the very least things get broken. You lose your temper, and unicorns get brushed." He shook his head, an affectionate twinkle in his eyes.

"I don't mind," Illium said with a wink.

"Well?" Joryn asked. "When is my execution?"

Kail laughed. "You really went off back there. I *never* saw that coming, Little Brother. I thought you were dead." He smiled lovingly at the young man brushing his unicorn friend. "But for the first time, I didn't even have to clean up after you with him. He raged in silence, clenched his fists, and I thought frantically how to talk you out of whatever punishment he was devising. Then he let out a breath and said, 'He's right.' "

Joryn looked up. "What?"

"He did, and then he got up and walked away."

"He fears me. That's why. You said so yourself."

"Agreed. Which is why you need to tread carefully now. You've tasted the benefits of another man's fear, but the other side is that—"

"He'll be plotting even harder to undo me behind the scenes. He'll be more subtle about hating me."

"I raised you well, Little Brother."

Both men laughed.

"But," Kail went on, "I can't warn you enough to be careful. It wouldn't be wise to repeat today's performance with Father any time soon, or ever."

"Why not?" Joryn demanded, suddenly the general again, brushing his war horse. "I don't serve him. He's a petty tyrant."

Astonished all over again, Kail said, "Because, he's the emperor of Nod and can make unthinkable trouble for you. Better to have him think you serve him. And why not? He's the *emperor* of Nod."

"I've come to a conclusion about that, Kail. I have vowed to serve Nod, and Nod is not this palace, nor the kingdom, nor the territory of the Empire, nor even the limitless terrain of the world called Nod. Nod is the people who inhabit this world, both in and beyond our empire. And I have said that my life belongs to them. My life belongs to Nod. So what I have realized is that one cannot always serve both a kingdom *and* its king. Sometimes, the service of one negates the other. Sometimes, in order to serve the kingdom, one must defy the king." He shook his head, the boy again. "Our father is not a man of the people. Feed them, shelter them, or kill them; it's all the same to him. I do not serve that man."

After a palpable silence, Kail said quietly, "I agree with you. And I'll do my best to protect you from him and the sycophants who might seek his favor at your expense. You have my word." He met Joryn's eyes, and both men smiled at the ease of their friendship.

"I want to go to the Whispering Plains," Joryn said then, changing the subject. "I want to see Galen again. No warriors, no conflicts, just me and Galen. And Illium of course."

"Of course," said the unicorn amiably.

"I'm pretty sure, for now anyway, you can write your own ticket," Kail said. "Father surely won't mind having you away from the palace."

"There's still the matter of Longshot's troubles," Joryn said. "He needs some help rescuing his girlfriend from some giant robots or something like that." Joryn laughed. "Of course it would have to be something like that. Anyway, we owe him, after all he did for us in Chiroptera. I'll help him with his problem, then I want to see Galen. I want to get away from here for just a little bit of time."

"I think that's a good idea, Joryn," Kail said. "You've definitely earned it. And you probably really need it after all of this. You need to unwind."

"Kail," Joryn said with deep sincerity, "thanks for always having my back."

The older prince smiled. "Always and forever, Little Brother."

EPILOGUE:
THE FATE OF NIGHTSTORM THE MERCILESS

ON THE OUTSKIRTS OF THE DARK FOREST, NIGHTSTORM foraged for food. His wound from the terrorbirds had not healed in the days since he'd been banished, and he was beginning to think he would, at long last, die; not in battle as he'd always dreamed, but in exile, scrounging like a beggar, sifting through the dirt for food, parched for blood.

"Nightstorm the Merciless," said a very deep and menacing voice. "I have a proposition for you."

The wounded, starving Chirop looked up to see a strong, hooded man, wearing a dark cape and an extraordinary horned mask. "That ... that mask!"

The man laughed, and there was nothing friendly about the sound. It was a sinister and predatory thing. "Yes, it is the mask you've only heard about in bedtime stories and nightmares."

Nightstorm considered this with a mixture of fear and dread. "*You* have a proposition? For me?"

"Yes. It occurs to me that you've been put in this position by the hated champion of Libran."

"Joryn of Nod," Nightstorm growled the name. "Yes. I was banished over his deal with the king."

"I've been watching you," the man said. "I've been watching many things. I can offer you a chance at revenge. I can offer you an opportunity to make both Joryn *and* King Orlok rue the day they ever crossed Nightstorm. I'm reorganizing, as it were. I'm returning to the foreground of history, and the Kingdom of Nod *will* be mine. I need warriors like you. Warriors with a grudge and the skills to back it up. Warriors who will *serve* me unquestioningly. Can you do this, Nightstorm?" The man, if such a term indeed applied to such a being, held out his hand and helped Nightstorm to his feet. "Can you become a servant of the Wanderer?"

Nightstorm hesitated for only a moment, then smiled nefariously. "It would be my honor, sir."

"*Master!*" the Wanderer corrected.

"Master," repeated the Chirop.

"Come then, Nightstorm. There is much to be done."

**The saga of *The Sword of Libran* will continue,
with Book III:
*Enter: The Wanderer***

ABOUT THE AUTHOR

Glenn Slade Clark, Jr. is the author of eight books, including the novel *Cry, Wolf: Shadow of the Werewolf*, the short fiction anthology *The Great Debate*, the Gothic horror series *The Chronicles of Nightfire, Texas*, and two fantasy series: *Metrognomes* and *The Legends of Nod*. He lives in Dallas, Texas, where he is currently hard at work on the next adventure in *The Legends of Nod*.

www.GlennSladeClarkJr.com

www.ingramcontent.com/pod-product-compliance
Lightning Source LLC
Chambersburg PA
CBHW060331260626
47160CB00007B/2760